About the Author

H. Eugene is an author and poet from Detroit, MI. He hopes that through his writing, he can reach and affect many. What you will find in his books is a renewed and fresh perspective of storytelling.

Please visit his website for information on exciting new projects at mrnovels.com

Also by H. Eugene

The Broken Microphone Trilogy
Book 1
Seri@l No Milk

Enter one rollercoaster of a thriller with Brooke Hannah's first adventure. You might want to leave the light on!

On December 12, 2012
Serial killer Thaddeus Gainsborough turns himself in and confesses to the grisly murders of eight missing people.
He is convicted and ordered to death by lethal injection in the swiftest trial in Florida history.
On the day of his execution, his final request will be granted ... An interview with Bay 9 News Reporter Brooke Hannah.
What ensues is a game of make-believe, unspeakable abuse, and psychological torture unlike anything she has ever experienced. Brooke is the key to something unmentionable!

How do you like your Seri@L? Milk or ... NO MILK

H. Eugene's first title

The Trifecta: God Will Never Forget This Day

Here are some of the reviews of this truly original and thoroughly entertaining novel.

"The Trifecta is well-written. A unique plot with intriguing characters. The story is an ingenious thriller that will captivate you. Well done!"

"Well written and based the most significant historical story ever written."

"A thought provoking read which ends with a sense of hope for the future despite the world's imperfections."

"This is a book that will make you think."

The Ugly Bomb

H. Eugene

The Broken Microphone Trilogy: The Ugly Bomb
Copyright © 2016 by H. Eugene

For information contact; mrnovels.com

ISBN:

ISBN-13:
Library of Congress Control Number:

Dear Reader,

Welcome back to the Broken Microphone Trilogy. I hope you enjoyed the first book in this trilogy, Seri@l No Milk. If you haven't read it yet you are in a for a treat.

The second book in this trilogy, The Ugly Bomb takes place nearly one year after her introduction to Mr. Gainsborough. In this story, she's about to unravel one of the greatest secrets in our recent history. It's a race against time as she tries to save us all from The Ugly Bomb. Now, get ready to be entertained.

Dedication

This book and this series is dedicated to my twin daughters, Brooke and Hannah. I love you both always and forever.

Acknowledgements

I would like to thank some individuals that helped to make this book a reality for me.

Tracee – thank you for all of your encouragement. I believe we have created a wonderful author tandem. On to the next!

Jill – I am completely humbled that you have read my work and have grown with me. Thank you for taking time out of your busy schedule to provide me with editing feedback.

K.D. – You my friend are amazing. You are truly an inspiration. Your editing abilities have enabled me to grow.

"I do not see why man should not be just as cruel as nature"
Adolf Hitler

Prologue

This is disgraceful." said Trekker. "How dare you come to me under false pretenses. I knew you weren't an investor of the arts. You lack refinement. You are wasting your time. I have nothing for you. I suggest you Google what you seek or go to one of the local libraries. Now, I'm going to have to ask you to leave. Please don't make me call the police."

Trekker places his hand on the phone to reinforce his threat.

"I wouldn't use that hand if I were you." said the stranger as he removes a pistol from his jacket pocket and screws on a silencer.

"You see, in my line of work I know when I'm being lied to. I also know how to get the answers I need. But in your case, I was given specific instructions. I ask you one question and await your response. If your response is not the right one, I get to plug some bullets in your sorry ass. Guess what? I didn't like your answer."

the stranger points his gun at Trekker.

"WAIT!" said Trekker as he tries to buy himself some time. "You don't understand. I do know her. I know her well."

"Oh, I'm aware of that. She died because of you. Enough talk… Goodbye!

Chapter 1

Homesick

So much has happened in the six months since Brooke Hannah's ascension to the spotlight. The biggest story of her career has people all over the country in a buzz. But some things automatically take the backseat to journalism or any career highlights.

It's been two days since Brook's mom called her to come home. Her dad is not doing well, but he is much too proud a man to admit it.

Time continues to stand still at the Hannah household. The same wonderful smell of lavender parades about the house. Everything looks just like the day they bought it. Her mom and dad loved to be neat and tidy, which is something that she's incorporated into her own habits.

There is one person obviously missing from the house. Against her mom's advice, Brooke's dad went to work anyway. Brooke and her mom have spent time catching up on current events since she arrived from the airport. There is anxious tension in the air, basically delaying the inevitable.

"Mom, what's wrong with dad?"

"So much has happened so quickly, honey. He is going to blow a gasket when he finds out you're here for this. For starters, his appetite has changed. You know how much your dad likes to eat. Now, eating twice a day seems to be just fine for him. He's sleeping a lot more than he used to. He seems so tired now. And just last week, his feet started to swell. He can't wear his dress shoes any longer, and he complains about his legs hurting. And lastly darling, he has been having problems urinating. It hurts him to go. He drinks plenty of water so that's certainly not the problem. He won't let me schedule a doctor's appointment. He keeps saying that *everything is fine,* but it's not."

"Who is his doctor, mom?"

"Dr. Williams, out of Henry Ford."

"Give me the number. I'm going to set up an appointment ASAP. And don't worry, I'll deal with his *fussin.*" Brooke said as they both laugh.

The next morning 10:14am Henry Ford Hospital

"My goodness dad, just relax. I know you don't think you need to be here, but we gotta get you well. I'm sure you'd like to go golfing with, Ernie, right? Well, we have to get that swelling down in those legs first. And how are you going to take mom ballroom dancing on those things anyway?"

Her dad cracks a smile.

"Alright all ready." said her dad. "I know I probably should have come sooner. I promised I wouldn't be like my own dad and be too proud to come to the hospital, but I guess I've done just that. I apologize to both of you for putting you through this. I just hate being a burden on anyone. And honey, I'm not mad at you for calling, Brooke. If I wasn't so darn stubborn I…"

"Mr. Hannah, you can come back now." interrupted the nurse. "You're going to be in room 3. I will get your weight and vitals in just a moment."

Mr. Hannah sees Dr. Williams who does a battery of tests, as Brooke and her mom anxiously await the results. After a couple of hours, the doctor gives them some news.

"Mrs. Hannah, I'll take you and your daughter to see your husband in a few moments." said Dr. Williams. "I have already explained our preliminary findings to your husband and wanted to do the same with both of you.

"First of all, we are going to be admitting him. He will probably need to be with us for at least a few days, maybe longer. Your husband has quite a bit of fluid on his lungs. Now, there are many causes for this, and I don't have the conclusive test results yet.

"Here's something that I can tell you. It appears that Mr. Hannah may have had several very minor heart attacks." Brooke and her mom gasp. "Please don't worry ladies. These attacks were so minor that he noticed them.

"Our first order of business is getting that excess fluid out of his system. That's going to take that swelling down. As far as the difficulty in urinating, those tests are still out. You did the right thing by getting him here when you did.

We can now get him treated and more importantly get him well again. Let's go and say hi to him."

After spending time getting her dad settled in a hospital room, Brooke and her mom go back home to get some of his essential items. She knows she would not be able to go back to Florida and function, so she takes a short leave from work.

The next couple of days finds her reacquainting herself with many friends and traveling to some of her favorite locations. During one of those afternoons, Dr. Williams calls her mom and asks if she and Brooke could meet with him and Mr. Hannah to discuss the results.

Brooke and her mom head quickly to the hospital. Both are concerned yet hopeful about the results. They meet the doctor in her dad's room.

"Thank you both for making it here so quickly, but as I said over the phone, there was no need for panic. The Lasix medication has worked quite well. There is almost no sign of swelling in his legs. Even his face looks a little better, don't you think?"

"I was telling him that yesterday, doctor." said Mrs. Hannah. "He looks so much better than when we brought him here."

"Yes, dad, I agree, you're looking like your old self again."

"I already went over these things with your husband. So, here's what we found. Mr. Hannah has been diagnosed with congestive heart failure. Now don't panic. Heart failure does not mean the heart has stopped working. Rather, it means that the heart's pumping power is weaker than normal. When you have heart failure, blood moves through the heart and body at a slower rate and pressure in the heart increases. As a result, the heart cannot pump enough oxygen and nutrients to meet the body's needs. His kidneys responded by retaining water. It can become *congested* in various parts of the body. For Mr. Hannah, it was his legs.

"As far as what caused this, there can be many explanations. One of them is having a heart attack, which it appears to have been the case several times, but on a much smaller scale.

"The good news is there are plenty of things you can do to improve your quality of life after heart failure. I'm going to go over those with you in detail. But before that, I want to discuss Mr. Hannah's problem with urination.

"I know this is going to seem like a throwing a lot at you, and not the news you want to here. Your husband has prostate cancer. The swelling of his prostate was causing pressure on his urethra, which in turn was causing him the discomfort. I know cancer is a scary word, but please know that this is not a period or an exclamation point. Rather, it can be the continuation of a very long life.

"Mr. Hannah will not have to do any chemotherapy. We can control this with over-the-counter medication, which is great news I'm sure you will agree. If your husband keeps up his exercise regimen, and continues to *watch* his diet, he will be with us for a very long time. Isn't that right, Mr. Hannah?"

"I suppose so, doc… I mean yes. Yes of course I'll be around. My wife wouldn't know what to do without all this handsomeness, and Brooke has crazy people coming after her. Somebody's gotta be there for them."

Before he can utter another word as everyone starts smiling…

"Can you excuse me for a moment, dad?"

"Yeah, sure honey. Are you OK?

"Yes, of course. I forgot I needed to have Charlie do something for me back at the station. I'll be back in a few moments."

Brooke leaves her father's room and retreats to the bathroom down the hall with swiftness and stealth. She locks the door behind her and paces for a moment.

Daddy…! Oh, God Dad.

The tears start rolling freely down her face.

I love you so much. I can't lose you. I just can't. What am I going to do? I can't leave you here like this. It's too much for mom. Dear God, I'm scared. OK… pull it together, girlie. No more tears. No more tears. We will figure this thing out as a family.

Brooke freshens up before returning to the room. The doctor gives them more information about her dad's treatment plan. They all embrace after the doctor leaves the room, vowing to face this as one solid unit… indeed as a family.

Chapter 2

Breaking News

December 14, 2015 Bay 9 News Office

The one thing Brooke doesn't miss about Detroit is the weather. With a nearly forty-degree difference in temperature, being back in her new home makes a lot of sense. But it's not about the weather on this particular day.

"Come on in, Brooke. My goodness, it's good to have you back," said Mr. Bergdoll as he extends his hand and then decides to give her a hug.

"It hasn't been the same without you around here. And poor Charlie's been looking like he lost his best friend. But enough of that. Please tell me how your dad is doing."

Brooke gives him the details of her dad's hospital stay and his next steps for recovery.

"Sir, if I may, can I be candid with you?"

"Brooke, I insist that you do."

"Thank you. When I saw my dad lying in that hospital bed with tubes inserted and machines humming, for the first time I saw my dad wasn't invincible. He was vulnerable like many of us. He was so vulnerable that he saw this as a burden. One that he didn't want to impart on anyone else.

"If my mother hadn't acted as she did…"

Brooke has to pause.

"Take your time Brooke. I understand... take your time."

"If she didn't act when she did, each day could have been more critical for him. I could have lost the most important man in my life. Age is that damned number that we can't change. We have to embrace it and enjoy all of its precious moments.

"My parents are aging and becoming more and more delightful. It's like enjoying them all over again, Mr. Bergdoll. I feel like this is my most important time to be with them. To help my mom look after my dad.

"This is where I'm torn, sir. This is where I need your help. Bay 9 News and St. Petersburg is my new home. Because of the courage of this news station, I was afforded a wonderful opportunity and a spectacular career. I am deeply indebted to this station for creating who I am professionally.

"But, my old home is calling me. The voice is so loud that I can't seem to hear anything else. In my heart I know my place is with my parents. And so here I am, hoping we can work out some type of solution."

"Brooke, you are so courageous. I deeply thank you for respecting me enough to be so candid. Allow me to return the favor.

"You've heard my boring history enough times. But there's something else woven in that history that not many know about. During my second year of grad school, my mother told me she was coming to visit. My mother *never* visited. I was so excited because she had never stepped foot on campus, and I was anxious to show her how I was living. She didn't believe in flying, so she took the bus. I picked her up from the bus terminal and off we went to lunch.

"It wasn't a pleasure visit. My mom told me that just a month before, she felt a lump on her breast and my dad took her to get it checked out. It was cancer. Cancer in an advanced stage. They would have to remove one of her breasts in order to save her life.

"Brooke, my mother and father were always an unbreakable foundation for me. When I looked into my mother's eyes that day, I could see the vulnerability in her just as you did with your dad. I left UCLA and finished my graduate program at the neighboring state college. It allowed me to be closer to my parents. I was home for dinner every day.

"Time is one of the most precious things that we have to offer. I believe it's time to spend and enjoy it with your parents."

"You have no idea how much I appreciate and respect you, sir. Thank you for sharing such a precious moment with me. So, what are my options? Where do I go from here?"

"When you told me you needed to high tail it back home, I was praying that everything would be alright with your dad; however, it also made sense for me to start exploring some options. I have already spoke with our HR Director. I put myself in your shoes, and I believe I have some options for you.

"First and foremost, you are eligible for FMLA and can certainly take advantage of that. But I have something that might be more appealing to you. You of course know Birdy Coswell?"

"Well, yes of course I do. She's the station manager at WDIV."

"Let's be honest here, Brooke. After the Gainsborough case, you are like national gold. You can go anywhere you want, and yes I already know that CNN contacted you."

He gives Brooke a wink. She's slightly embarrassed and looks down smiling.

"But I also know you turned it down, as well as turning down at least a dozen business lunches. Yes, news travels fast. I spoke with Birdy while you were gone, and she has an investigative reporter spot waiting for you if you are interested.

"You would get to keep the same pay, and your personal days and vacation would be matched. So, what do you think about that so far?"

"My goodness, sir, I am completely floored. I certainly didn't expect anything like this. It's wonderful. I love the idea and am extremely grateful that you went above and beyond for me. I…"

"I'm not done working my magic yet, Brooke. There's more. I know a certain person that has family in Michigan. This certain person and his wife just came back a few months ago from Traverse City. This person and his wife have been talking about moving back for a little while now."

"Sir, you're talking about Charlie!?"

"That's right. If you are interested, a package deal has already been arranged. You get to take your cameraman with you. What good is a reporter without her right hand?"

"OMG sir. Really? Truly?"

Brooke jumps out of her seat and gives Mr. Bergdoll a huge hug.

"Sir, I accept. Thank you so much for making this happen for me. I am forever grateful to this station for everything."

"It's my pleasure, and I'm glad to hear that. Please know that you will always have a spot waiting for you here whenever and if you decide you want to come back.

"If you can give me about ten days to wrap some things up and transition around here, we can have you back home in mid-January. Now get out here and go do some reporting. And go find that sorry camera man of yours. He needs that smile put back on his face."

"Yes sir, you got it!"

Chapter 3

Detroit Style

February 14, 2016 Valentine's Day

Brooke has officially settled back home in the Motor City. As much as her parents lamented her leaving for Florida, they fought her tooth and nail about coming back. They wanted Brooke to stay in Florida and continue to build on her career and potentially move to an even larger news market.

Brooke's conversation with Mr. Bergdoll was all the fuel she needed to know she was making the right decision. She wasn't back home because she felt her parents needed her. She came back because she needed them.

Charlie and his family had an easy time moving in and gearing up. Work at WDIV was a much different change of pace for both Brooke and Charlie. Here in Detroit, there was a sense of connectedness with the community that was refreshing, though challenging. She was quickly able to build several important relationships in her short period back home.

Her new colleagues and station manager were all extremely supportive and welcoming. This was indeed her new home. It was Detroit that she needed. And on this Valentine's Day, these created memories will never fade.

5:35pm BB's Diner

If there is one place that can never be avoided for Brooke, its BB's Diner. She fell in love with this place years ago and became great friends with the owner. Whenever she visits, he makes her a special steak and shrimp dish that's not posted on the menu.

"Oh no! Oh Nooo! Please tell me that's not Hollywood Hannah Banana." said BB the owner, as Brooke makes her way inside.

"BB!" shouted Brooke as she runs up and hugs him.

He always lifts her up off the ground.

"My goodness lady, look at you. That Florida sun has made you even prettier. And boy I gotta tell you, my mouth flew open when they made that announcement on Channel 4. It's good to have you back, Hannah Banana. So, what's new with you, lady? Can I put together your favorite?"

"You know good and well that I'm dying for my fav. I couldn't wait to get here. Things are going good. I'm settled in and getting my *Detroit legs* back!"

"Well amen to that. And I won't bring up that psycho from Florida, but let's just say I'm glad to have you in my presence again. I was ready to come down there and take care of dude. Don't mess with my girl."

"Thank you ,BB. You are so sweet."

"Hey, come on back. You can relax in the office while I prepare your dish. How's mom and dad doing? And this is V-Day missy. Why are you here? I'm sure the line of guys praying for a chance with all that gorgeousness, is miles and miles long."

"Ha ha, and whatever to that. The folks are both doing quite well... hold on BB, I need to take this call."

"Take it in the office."

"Hello, Brooke Hannah."

"Good evening, Miss Hannah. My name is Peter Heidle. I am the personal attorney and friend to Mr. Hans Albrecht. Surely you know the name."

"Wait--Mr. Albrecht... yes, sure I do. He's a huge developer. So how may I help you Mr. Heidle? Did the station give you this number?"

"Mr. Albrecht made a special request to your station manager. They are good friends. But enough of this small chatter. The reason for my call is to request your audience. You see, Mr. Albrecht doesn't have much longer to live. We are probably talking days at this point. He personally requested me to reach out to you. There is something he wants to discuss with only you. Can you drop by his residence this evening, say around 9pm?"

Brooke hesitates as a familiar euphoria overcomes her. She looks over at BB as he continues to prepare her favorite dish. He smiles at her and proceeds.

"Sure, Mr. Heidle. I would be honored to meet Mr. Albrecht. 9pm is fine."

"Wonderful, Miss Hannah. He will be pleased to know that you accepted his invitation. I will send you the address information to your phone. Until later."

"Everything ok, Hannah Banana? You look a little flustered."

"No, I'm good. Duty always calls." she said as flashes a radiant smile. "Where's my food, dude?"

BB laughs. "Did you want to take this with you, or do you want to chill out a minute with your good bud?"

"Pass me the plate and pass me the utensils. That smells way too amazing to be wrapped up."

Chapter 4

Nighttime Confessions

8:55pm Albrecht Mansion

Hans Albrecht came to Michigan in the late 60's via a personal request from the governor who deeply admired and respected his architectural work in California. By the late 70's Hans had started his own acquisition and development company. By 1983 he was on Forbes list for the top ten wealthiest in America. Today, he is the 7th richest person in the world.

His contributions to Michigan are innumerable, particularly his investments in the City of Detroit in recent years. He is lauded around the world for his humanitarian efforts and respected by those in very high places.

Hans married only once, and that was to the love of his life, Earla Dennis. They had two children together, both boys. One day while on her way back home from the college dorm shopping with her sons, a sleeping truck driver swerved into their lane. She and the boys were killed instantly.

Hans never remarried and was never quite the same after the terrible tragedy. He turned over the reins of leadership at his company and began traveling. Though still very active in the running of the company and his humanitarian causes, he slowly stepped away from the limelight.

Brooke pulls up to the gated property. Before she can exit her vehicle to push the intercom, the tremendous gate slides open. As she pulls forward, she marvels at the expanse and beauty of his mansion.

Hans built this mansion with his own design. Reminiscent of an old Hollywood home, the entrance is made of beautifully sculpted glass. There is a full-scale Greek statue that can be seen sitting just behind the door.

Surely when a man such as Hans has amassed so much, there are certain corners that are best left darkened. Brooke was about to bring light to one of them.

"Miss Hannah, welcome to the Albrecht residence," said Mr. Heidle as he invites her in. "You continue to exude professionalism and courtesies many take for granted. I truly appreciate your promptness.

"I'm afraid things have taken a turn for the worse with Mr. Albrecht. The doctor is upstairs with him now. He says it would be a miracle if he made it through the night. His mind is still sharp and agile. It's his body that is refusing to cooperate. But we don't have time for the minor details. He's been asking for you. We should go now."

Mr. Heidle leads her upstairs to Mr. Albrecht's room. The doctor dismisses himself. As Brooke enters the room, she sees Mr. Albrecht sitting up comfortably in his bed. Though he's 89 years of age and about to make his transition from this world, he still looks remarkable and pleasant. She cannot help but to respect the peace she sees in his eyes.

Speaking in a broken German accent.

"It is indeed a pleasure to lay my eyes on something so beautiful." he said as he extends his hand. "A fitting way to leave this cold and confused place."

"Why thank you for the kind compliment, Mr. Albrecht. It is a pleasure to meet you."

"Peter, please leave us now dear friend. Go and pour yourself a brandy and kick your feet up. There is much work ahead of you."

Mr. Heidle exits the room.

"Miss Hannah, please pull over that chair. There are some things I want to bore you with."

Brooke pulls over the wonderfully adorned Victorian styled chair.

"I have a reputation for being very direct and to the point. The short of why you are here is this. I am dying and I want to bear my soul. I picked you because of your work with that dreadful Gainsborough case. In particular, I thoroughly respect how you've handled yourself and your celebrity since then. Something tells me others would have handled themselves quite differently if faced with the same set of circumstances.

"Gainsborough is as much a revolutionary hero, as he is a sadistic killer. This is not the first time we've seen that scenario, however. So, my respect and high degree of trust is why you are standing here. I believe you are going to make great things happen in this world. In fact, you already are."

"Mr. Albrecht, I truly appreciate your confidence and respect. I take those things to heart. Please tell me how I can be of assistance."

"Very well… let's switch gears and slow it down a little bit. It's time for that boring part of the conversation. Tell me the truth, how much did you like history when you were in school."

Brooke smiles.

"Honestly, there were a few things that really captured my imagination, but overall, it was just OK."

"What do you think about World War II?"

"The world certainly had a lot going on at that time. The Germans and the Russians, the Japanese and the Americans… millions of lives lost. A truly dark moment in human history."

"Indeed, you are right, Miss Hannah. A truly dark moment it was. Part of my history that is widely unknown is that I was a participant in WWII. I was just old enough to join, and I surely had purpose."

Before he could continue, he coughs violently. The well-placed handkerchief over his mouth can't quite conceal the innocence of blood.

"Would you like me to get the doctor, Mr. Albrecht?"

He gestures no as he regains his composure.

"I'm fine now, but if you don't mind, can you pour me a glass of water from over at the dresser?"

"Sure." Brooke rises to get the water.

"One more thing, Miss Hannah. Don't tell the doc, but if you look just inside that top drawer beneath the undershirts, you'll find a most delightful flask. Can you bring that as well?"

Brooke smiles as she finds the monogrammed flask. She brings both to him.

"Are you a drinker, Miss Hannah?"

"I do partake every now and again, sir."

After drinking his water, he unscrews the cap from his flask, taking a long pause before a carefully drawn sip.

"This is handmade bourbon. Bottled in 1982 in Amsterdam. There were only 6 bottles made. This is bottle number three. Sadly, there are only a few more sips left. But how fitting for me.

"Ah, you must excuse me. I'm an old man and I sometimes tend to ramble on and on about nothing. Now where were we before my coughing fit? Oh yes, WWII. It was 1941 and the world seemed at the point of spontaneous combustion. There I was 18 years old and on the front lines with the German Army.

"I remember the first time I met the Fuhrer, Adolf Hitler. He was wildly imaginative and captivating. It only took moments for his charisma to rope you in to his ideologies. Did I agree with them all? No. Do I believe that millions of people deserved to die so maliciously? No. But the war was not just about beliefs. It was about treachery and arrogance veiled in humility.

"The war was about *quid pro quo*. It was about the biggest set and gamble in our young history. Hitler was portrayed as a tyrant, but there was so much more to the story. He was also the persecuted."

Brooke looks somewhat baffled, as she repositions herself in the chair.

"I see that look on your face, Miss Hannah and I know it well. It is a reflection of what mine looked like when I was exposed to the truth. It is something I've been carrying around for over 70 years. I refuse to die knowing such things without bringing them to light."

Mr. Albrecht goes into another coughing fit, this time more blood escapes from his handkerchief. He motions to Brooke to stay seated. He eventually regains his composure. His face has become a shade lighter.

"I look at you, and I see beauty and youth. I see so much talent and promise. The world deserves a second chance. The world deserves to know the truth. I want you to expose it. Expose it with bravery and unabashed resiliency. You have momentum and respect in your favor. The world will trust your character. I want you to stop the terror from happening."

"What terror Mr. Albrecht? What truth am I to expose? Are you sure I'm the right person you seek?"

"I have read before that some have such a heightened sense of clarity right before they die. I have never felt clearer in mind and purpose. You must find a way to destroy *The Ugly Bomb*. The production is…"

"The ugly bomb!?" quipped Brooke as she looks completely befuddled.

"Please go to Barnaby Trekker."

"Wait. *Barnaby Trekker*!? I know him. He was a good friend of my grandfathers. He runs the Holocaust Museum in Farmington Hills. What does he have to do with this?"

Mr. Albrecht smiles at Brooke and pauses. His head slouches over. Brooke rises slowly as she walks over to him, already knowing the answer to the question. Mr. Albrecht had passed away. She exits the room and makes her descent down the stairs where she makes eye contact with the doctor. They both nod at each other without exchanging words. Mr. Heidle emerges from the great room.

"So, it is done, Miss Hannah? My friend has made his transition?"

"Yes, Mr. Heidle, I'm afraid so. But he died peacefully. He enjoyed the last of his hand made bourbon."

Mr. Heidle and the doctor both smile.

"I always knew about that flask." said the doctor. "I just decided to let him indulge. It was one of the few things that brought him happiness."

"Agreed." said Mr. Heidle. "So, Miss Hannah. I am hopeful that before Hans passed away, he was able to relieve himself of the burden he's been carrying around. Please know that whatever it was, he did not share it with anyone. You are held in high regard. You are in unfamiliar territory. I hope you are able to give my friends transition an exclamation point."

"I am humbled by being here and sharing his last moments, Mr. Heidle. I'm not sure what I'm to do next but rest assured that Mr. Albrecht will have eternal peace where he is going."

Chapter 5

In Moderation

9:30am WDIV station manager's office

C ome on in, Brooke. Close the door. I am so excited right now I'm ready to burst," said Mrs. Coswell. "I received a call late last night from a very good friend with the Committee on Presidential Debates. So, you know the first presidential debate is scheduled for September 26th at Wright State University, right?"

"Yes, sure I do Mrs. Coswell. I believe the whole world will be watching this one. Sim City fever is unreal right now. Wait a minute why are you excited? Are you going to let me cover it?"

Brooke is excited without hearing the rest of what Mrs. Coswell had to say.

"No Brooke, I'm sorry to bust your bubble, but you won't be able to cover the debate."

Brooke's smile disappears.

"The call from Mr. Learer last night was asking permission to see you if you would *moderate* the first debate."

"What!? Wait… me moderate? No way Are you serious right now?"

"I am very serious, Brooke. Evan Parker had to withdraw for personal reasons. They really want to shake up this debate. They want someone trustworthy and credible. Your name was at the top of that very short list. This is a tremendous career pat on the back. So, what do you think? Are you in?"

"Oh my God, Mrs. Coswell, I can't believe I'm having this conversation right now. Of course, I'm in. But wait, are you sure you want to endorse me for something like this? Every one of the journalists chosen have decades of experience and respect. I have never done anything like this. I don't want to say I'm out of my league, but…"

"You were handpicked by a committee that heavily weighed you against all of the top journalists in the country. Unanimously, each committee member picked you. You are not outclassed Brooke, and that is the last time I ever want doubt to creep into your mind. You are in a class by yourself. You are young, ambitious, full of fire, and you are a woman garnering the respect of those that used to turn their noses up. You are more than ready for the challenge. Now, shall I tell Mr. Learer that you accept?"

"Thank you for the speech, Mrs. Coswell. My dad would have said exactly the same thing. You two are so much alike. I enthusiastically accept."

"Good. I am so excited, Brooke. This is a wonderful opportunity for you, this station, and the city. I'm going to have you partner with Debbie. She has lots of debate coverage experience. We will make sure you are incredibly prepared for September."

"Umm, Mrs. Coswell, just one question… can I take Charlie with me?"

"How did I know that was coming? I'm sure that can be worked out, Brooke. Now back to work. We have stories to cover."

"Yes ma'am!" Brooke smiles as she resists the temptation to run through the office screaming.

Chapter 6

War Causalities

Holocaust Memorial Center, Farmington Hills

The holocaust center is run by longtime supporter and major financial backer, Barnaby Trekker. Mr. Trekker is an Auschwitz concentration camp survivor. His book on the atrocities of the holocaust netted him 37 weeks on the New York Times Best Seller List.

He has been a staunch supporter of human rights and welfare. He became lifetime best friends with Brooke's grandfather after the war. He has followed her career with much pride and interest. Little did he know her visit wasn't merely for pleasure.

"Well, will you look at this beautiful blossom." said Mr. Trekker. "My goodness, I haven't seen you since when? High school? Has it really been that long?"

"Yes, I'm afraid so." said Brooke as they both embrace. "You continue to defy time. You look great, and this place is amazing. I'm sorry I didn't come by sooner to visit. And please accept my condolences for Netta. She taught me so much growing up. I do miss her. I didn't hear the news till after the funeral. Did you receive my card and letter?"

"I sure did, Brooke, and I thank you humbly for such a heartfelt message. I miss her dearly. My daughter fought with courage and humility to the very end. She is now somewhere enjoying ice cream socials with her mother. But enough of that. This is your first time here. Allow me to give you a tour."

"Mr. Trekker, I would love to go on a tour, but perhaps some other time. I'm going to have to get back to work in a little bit. Do you have somewhere we can talk privately?"

"Well sure, Brooke. Heavens, this sounds so official. We can speak discreetly in my office. Right this way."

As Brooke follows a step behind Mr. Trekker, she questions where this visit will lead her.

"Please have a seat and make yourself comfy. Can I get you anything to drink? I also have some homemade sugar cookies. If memory serves, you and Netta used to fight over them all the time."

"You have *sugar cookies*? Did you make them?"

"I wouldn't have it any other way."

"Then yes, please allow me to indulge." she said as her smile lights up the room.

As she reaches into the tin canister, Mr. Trekker lights up.

"Brooke, does this visit have anything to do with the millage we are trying to get passed?"

"No, it does not. I am aware of the millage, however. I believe its money well spent… just my opinion."

"Well, that's good to know. We are going to have a fight on our hands getting this thing passed, but I'm confident we will. So, tell me, what's on your mind?"

"I visited Hans Albrecht a couple days ago before he passed away."

"You visited Hans!?" Mr. Trekker sits back in his chair. "Wait. Why were you visiting him? So, this is the purpose of your visit?"

"Mr. Albrecht's personal friend and attorney, Mr. Heidle, requested me to attend his mansion. I was there with Mr. Albrecht when he spoke his last words. Before he expired, he made reference to, *The Ugly Bomb*. He asked me to seek you out. I don't believe he knew that we were already very well acquainted. What is an ugly bomb?"

Mr. Trekker's face turns instantly pale.

"Dear God," he said as he slowly rises from his chair. "I have not heard that name in a very long time, Brooke. Please, I must ask that you forget you ever heard about such a thing. There can be no good in snooping around with this. With all due respect, this is way out of your league, young lady. You have no idea what will surround you if you choose to flip on the light switch of this subject."

"Mr. Trekker, you know you have my utmost respect. I am not here to create some type of story. I really have no idea why I'm seeking you out. He told me that he trusted me with this information. He told me this bomb, or whatever it is needed to be destroyed. He made references to WWII. If you tell me this is a non-issue, I will forget we ever had this conversation and move on."

"It's more than a non-issue. It's a catastrophe looming. It waits for instructions. Perhaps it's your journalistic voice that was the appeal. Maybe Hans thought you could expose and air out the world's dirty laundry. If you want to hear this story, I'm afraid you will be late getting back to work."

"That's quite alright. I am actually doing some research today. I can make the time."

"Good! I need you to write something down before I tell you a story."

Brooke reaches into her bag and removes her planner and pen.

"I wrote three books, but only published two of them. The third book was made up of poems. When I was in Auschwitz, I found a piece of coal. I used that coal to write my thoughts on a raggedy t-shirt that I kept hidden inside my pants. Each day I wondered if I would live to see the next. Each day, I wrote as if my life was full of promise and splendor. That's what gave me hope.

"Years later after I survived the camp, I transferred all of those thoughts to paper. Those thoughts, or poems to be more precise were set to be published. I'm still not quite sure how, but my poems made it all the way to the desk of Stalin. He was intrigued by one poem in the book. The one titled *T.U.B.* We were liberated, so to speak, by the United States, Great Britain, UN Forces, and Russia. For some time, I was in East Germany, which was then the Soviet Occupation Zone. There are more stories I could tell you about that, but once again I'm getting ahead of myself.

"The poem I wrote was cryptic yet menacing. Stalin felt threatened by it, yet he didn't firmly understand why. Had he known the true underlying theme, I would have surely been killed. There was only one other person that knew the true meaning of the poem. That person was Hans Albrecht. We met in Auschwitz. He was a soldier, and there I was the garbage.

So, this Hans guy was a Nazi. This is getting weird.

"He was only in that particular camp twice. On that first day, he exposed me for concealing the writing on the undershirt. But he didn't turn me in. He read everything I wrote. He nearly wept. He told me I was a great writer and encouraged me to continue. He hated the war and what was being done to so many innocent people. He told me if we both made it out alive, we should look each other up and connect again.

"The other German soldiers and guards were so pompous and arrogant. They said many things in front of us that should never have been shared. Many of them stopped resorting to whispering, because according to one them, we would never live to tell the stories anyway. From their lips I heard the rumors. From their lips I heard about things that even they were shocked to hear, yet they remained fascinated all the same. These conversations also gave me additional material to fuel my writing.

"Years later, Hans and I reunited. We shared each other's stories, along with the most shocking revelations that my ears had been privy to. We couldn't tell anyone outright what we learned after putting our heads together. No one would have believed us. Besides, it would more than likely mean instant death to us and our families.

"Can you imagine me wanting to take such risks after just surviving that concentration camp nightmare? I embedded certain revelations and secrets in the poem T.U.B. The acronym stood for The Ugly Bomb. I was such a coward, I should have stood up to Stalin, but at what price. The poem is even more relevant now as it was almost 70 years ago. Needless to say, the book nor poem ever made it to the light of day. Write this down Brooke:

> *Death is elusive in fair trade*
> *The twin faces mark a new day*
> *The way of the sun will be drowned in ashes*
> *The wall of purpose was never weak, only invisible*
> *The tri-colored soldiers convey arrogance*
> *The voice of reason will ignite the switch*
> *The world will lay flat from treachery*
> *The ugly bomb may now rest*

"And so there you have it. The poem that has led you here. Please tell me Brooke, what else did he mention?"

"Nothing really. He was just as cryptic as your poem. He told me that the world deserved a second chance, and that the world deserved to know the truth. He wants me to expose it. He actually said, *Expose it with bravery and unabashed resiliency*. He believes the world will have this high level of trust in me. I have a moral compass like so many others, Mr. Trekker. I am certainly not beyond criticisms."

"Indeed, you are not. Everyone in your profession has a moral compass. But yours is locked in only one direction... the right direction. My friend chose you wisely. In light of our conversation, I will need to cut it short. There are some things I need to mull over. I will be leaving at the end of the week for Europe. I won't be back until sometime in late August. Fear not, you may continue doing things as if this conversation never transpired.

"There is nothing more you can do at this point. That does not preclude me, however. No, I have some things that I need to gather together for you. Going to Europe allows the perfect window of opportunity. I will be in touch.

"Oh, but wait. There are some things that I'd like you to read. One of them is a journal that I kept while I lie a prisoner in that death camp. It will give you an eye-opening account of what things were really like there. The other letter I received from one of the SS soldiers at Auschwitz. I believe the letter will draw a picture of some of the resentment coming from Hitler's own party near the end. He mentioned that a copy of the same had gone to the Americans, though he didn't say who specifically. To this day, I still don't understand why I was the recipient of it. Some things we don't question; we just accept them. It was really great seeing you again. Please take care."

As Brooke leaves the museum, she glances back at her notes, and the other information Mr. Trekker had given her, more particularly the T.U.B. Poem.

What the heck am I getting myself in to? I should have just been an actress. I feel like I'm in Hollywood.

Chapter 7

The Persecuted

After a long day, Brooke returns home with the earlier conversation with Mr. Trekker fresh on her mind. As she makes some hot tea, she settles down in her chaise to read the journals that she was given. She starts with Mr. Trekker's.

June 2, 1944 Auschwitz Concentration Camp

I have already written many things. This journal is one that I hoped I would never have to start, but things seem daunting... I am losing hope. Perhaps someone will find this along with the rest of my work. If you are reading this, I hope you are safe and not another victim of these unspeakable atrocities. But, if you are like me, please continue to fight. Fight with all that you have left. I must go now. Time to remove more bodies. I shall journal again soon.

June 5, 1944

I've been too weak to even write. But I must push on. This is the third day without food or water. The German women soldiers are drinking wine and in a drunken state, as they take whips to the frail backs of those poor children. My heart weeps for that little girl. I believe she's only five.

June 26, 1944

I have dragged fifteen dead bodies from the hut and added them to the stack. I was rewarded with a piece of bread and a cup of water. It was my first meal and drink in two days. The SS Soldiers are deviants. They brought in full-length mirrors and made many of us look at our naked bodies in front of it. Those that were too weak to stand in front of the mirror were beaten, tortured, or burned. Six of them didn't make it.

July 6, 1944

Something is happening. They need more able-bodied workers. I have eaten for three days straight. My mind feels good, but my body still does not want to cooperate. Although the food has helpful, I am unable to stand much longer than a few minutes. If I don't get my strength back, I know they will put me in the gas chamber.

December 27, 1944

I feared that my work… all my writing had been lost. But it was simply moved to another hut by another fellow prisoner who knoweth not whom they belonged to. Thank goodness he and I shared some stories. His mention of the poems was a Godsend. I'm not sure how much more I will be able to write. In a few days they want us all to march somewhere. They won't give us any details. So many have already died, and many more won't make the trip, I'm sure of it. We haven't eaten in nearly five days and haven't had drinking water in nearly two. I've lost count of how many of us they have been sent to the gas chamber. There are so many bodies lying around. They have made us to look like decorations for the ground. I can't cry anymore. I no longer feel anything.

December 31, 1944

I have heard the soldiers whispering. The allied forces are drawing near. They are hauling us away from here tomorrow. I won't go... I can't go. I am going to bury myself under the mound of dead corpses nearest to the third hutch by the entrance. Is it too late?

Chapter 8

Am I a Monster?

Brooke can't tear herself away from what she's reading. After reading Mr. Trekker's journal, she opens the letter from the SS Officer.

February 17, 1944

Dear sir,

I have been stationed here at Auschwitz for nearly two months now. This is my second camp, the first being Bergen-Belsen. My purpose for writing this letter is to seek amnesty and to provide my immediate surrender to your soldiers. This war is not something we can win. It is no longer anything I want to win.

I have walked down paths where thousands of bodies line them like overstocked toys. I have been around so much death that I can no longer feel anything. My fellow officers walk around not oblivious… no. They see what they've done. They see the starving people. They've beat them, shot them, and dragged them to the gas chambers when the Jews were unable to walk on their own. They no longer care. These lives mean nothing to them.

The Fuhrer has taught us that the Jews, homosexuals, Jehovah's Witnesses, the weak, and the handicapped are nothing but burdens on what otherwise would be a perfect society. He has taught us the Germans of the pure Aryan Race are the answer to the world. I believed it at first, I will admit, but that little boy... that little boy broke me. The little kid was barely able to stand. He had been starved to the point of near death. He reached out to my pant leg and told me to smile. He said he knew that he was dirty and didn't deserve to live anymore. He wanted me to know he wasn't mad at anyone. He said he was ready. He asked me to please help him leave and he managed to smile at me. I couldn't do it, but the other officer who overheard the conversation withdrew his pistol quickly and shot the boy in his head.

When that happened, everything started to make sense to me. Am I a monster for standing by and watching this needless slaughter day after day? I will let you make that decision. There are others who are ready to defect. You shall hear from us again shortly. May God have mercy on everyone in this damned place.

TC

Brooke folds the letter back slowly. Reading about these atrocities through the eyes of those present is heart-wrenching. She wonders what Mr. Trekker will bring before her the next time.

Chapter 9

Full Plate

May and the colorful spring in Michigan cannot be denied for its subtle beauty. Remnants of winter are all gone and the multiplicity of colors and the smell of fresh clippings assume and replicate. Amongst this sophistication of arrangements lie a complicated formula. Complication that mirrors the many thoughts going through Brooke's mind.

Brooke and Charlie are at the end of another day, as they park at Belle Isle Park and have a chat.

"Can you believe it's been five months already?" Asked Charlie. "Lori is totally loving her graphics design job, and guess what? They're going to let her work remote from home four days out of the week. This has turned out to be a very good move. And I have to admit, our news team has been nothing but supportive. I feel like I never left Florida.

"You and I spend so much time on our cell phones and laptops that we haven't caught up in a bit. Plus, you're like Miss Superstardom now. Do I have to pay you admission for a chat?"

They both laugh.

"Nooo, Charlie, geez! You know... I was just thinking the same thing. Five months have come quickly. There has been so much going on. And since you also started working with Quinn, I guess we haven't chatted in a while.

"I'm worried about my dad, Charlie. That was a scary incident last month. It really shot my nerves."

"Wait, you had started to tell me about it, then we got sidetracked. What exactly happened with your dad?"

"So, he was still having problems with going to the bathroom and urinating. My mom called and asked if I could stop by after work. When I got there, my dad was sitting in the living room in a chair my mom brought up from the basement. He was more comfortable sitting in it for long periods of time.

"He said his legs hurt a little bit, but he couldn't move them. His eyes Charlie... he just didn't look good. I asked him if he wanted to get some fresh air, and he nodded yes. When I tried to help him up, his legs just gave. My mother and I were holding him up, but his legs were just gone, non-functional. Then he started nodding off. I had to keep waking him back up after we sat him back down in the chair.

"I asked mom about his medicine, but she was nervous. She didn't understand what was happening. We called the ambulance and got him to the hospital. We met with his doctor the next day. They found a blockage in his bladder that required surgery. The blockage had given him an infection. The infection spread to his legs, making them inoperable.

"The surgery was successful, and my dad was back to his old self with the exception of one thing, he couldn't walk on his own anymore. He had to go through weeks of physical therapy to retrain himself on how to walk. He now has a walker and needs assistance going up and down the stairs. My dad has been so independent all these years. It's so hard to see him like he is now."

"Brooke, I'm so sorry to hear about this. It seems like he is on the path to recovery though. Having you here is making a huge difference. I'm sure of it."

"Thank you, Charlie. One day at a time, right? And I'm trying not to, but I'm stressing a little bit over this presidential debate. It's four months away, but it seems like it's only weeks. There is still so much preparation. But I gotta tell you, my support from our news family has been astounding. I will be well prepared, I'm sure. But you know me, I love to have all the finite details nailed."

"Yeah, I know Miss Perfection." he said as he gives her a fist pump. "We are in this together. It will all work out, kiddo."

"Speaking of *being in this together*, I wanna ask you a question."

"Sure… go for it!"

"Can you tell me what the difference is between my life this past year, and a movie script?"

"Hmmm. I suppose the only difference is that yours is reality, and you can't do a retake. Once the action starts, it doesn't stop until… *it stops*."

"OK, then brace yourself, buddy!"

"Oh no, not again, Brooke. What are you up to know?"

"I honestly have no idea, maybe nothing, but I'm sure it will come full circle soon."

"Umm, what the heck is that supposed to mean? Another Serial killer or lunatic?"

"I don't believe either of those, Charlie. This one seems more conspiracy related. Something that might be incredibly newsworthy. I will keep you posted. I feel more like a private detective than a reporter.

"Well, that's the beauty of what you do. You can blend reporting with detective work so to speak. Just be careful and none of these lone cowboy... err, I mean cowgirl missions. And while we are on the subject of reporting, I need to ask you a question."

"Oh boy, here we go. OK, Charlie, what is it?"

"Simon City is speaking at Cobo Hall and has that place jammed. He's giving our station an exclusive interview, something he's been shying away from on the campaign trail so far. You were handpicked to moderate in September. Why wouldn't you be the person doing this exclusive? It just doesn't seem to flow right in my head."

Brooke sighs.

"That mind of yours is always turning. I'm going to tell you this and you better not breathe a word of it."

"I promise. This conversation will not leave this van."

"Good. Simon City's campaign manager did contact me about doing an exclusive."

"I knew it!"

"Easy, Charlie, Geez. Something came to me quickly when I was asked to do the interview. I thought about the ratings for our morning show, and how they slipped due to that erroneous information we received. Sasha took the fall for that, and I don't believe it was fair. An exclusive interview with Simon City would provide a huge boost to the show's ratings and give her back that credibility she unfairly lost. I asked them to contact Mrs. Coswell and let them know they wanted to do the morning show. His campaign manager didn't know the details, but somehow understood. The rest is history."

"This is the Brooke Hannah many get to know. You are a huge cream puff. But you know what, I respect the hell out of you. You make me proud to be your friend."

"Enough of this deep stuff, Charlie. Let's grab some ice cream before we head back. I need to bury my mind in confectionary heaven for a few moments."

Chapter 10

It begins

July 16, 2016 9:40am

Brooke's cell phone rings as she sits reading and enjoying her cup of special blend Earl Grey. She looks at the caller id and sees a name that makes her smile anxiously.

"Good morning, Mr. Trekker. Oops, I suppose it's afternoon where you are. How are you doing?"

"No, good morning is appropriate. I'm back home now. I needed to cut my trip short."

"I'm sorry to hear that. Is everything fine?"

"Yes, of course. I need to meet with you. Are you available today or tomorrow?"

"Sure. I have some errands to run today, but Sunday should be a rather low maintenance day. What time is good for you?"

"If you could meet me back here at the museum around 11:00am that would be great. I really appreciate this, Brooke."

"No problem at all. See you in the morning."

As Brooke hangs up, she's starting to have that movie script feeling overcome her.

This should be interesting.

The next morning 11:00am

"Brooke, thank you for joining me today. The museum is closed to visitors for the next couple of days as we put the finishing touches on our addition. We are the only two in this lonely place right now. I cut my trip short because of some troubling developments. Some of these developments are ones I'm sure Hans would have spoken of had he not expired suddenly. I also fear that I may be running out of time.

"Running out of time!? How so, Mr. Trekker?"

"Japan is making credible threats against our recent policies. Russia is pissed at us for our interference in Syria, and our lack of support against IS. And let us not talk about spies. First, we have yet another covert coward leaking secrets of intelligence and being offered asylum in Russia. Then, our own leaked spy protocol involving the German Chancellor. Our countries are on the brink of a melting point.

"And here is an interesting fact for you, Brooke. Japan, Russia, Germany, and the United States were once the key members of an off the record historic event nearly 80 years ago. One that unraveled quickly. And now history is about to repeat itself."

"Wait! So, this has to do with the possibility of another war?"

"It is indeed about another war, Brooke. Perhaps WWIII is much closer than we think. Each of these countries have in their arsenal one weapon that can change the face of mankind. The ugly bomb or bombs are Grade X weaponry, which I will explain to you momentarily. We are on the brink of war, but our enemy can be one or many. It's not just about the United States, it's about the entire world. One of these ugly bombs can change history forever. But who will be the person or country to bring about the destruction of this world? The weapons and the plot must be exposed. These bombs must be destroyed before they can ever be deployed.

"This I believe is how you will aide us. But before we can proceed with this current conversation, I feel you must understand one crucial point of unknown chaos and mystery. I must educate you properly on the Fuhrer. History is quite wrong."

Chapter 11

Backdoor Agreements

September 1st 1938 Paris, France

The office of French President Albert Lebrun was thick with the smell of cigar smoke and the velvetiness of imported whiskey. The president was the mediator and witness to the largest agreement ever reached between Japan, Russia, Germany, and the United States. The president lays out the details of the agreement in his native language as each translator engages their leader.

"Let it be duly noted that on this day September 1, 1938 that Germany has in principle agreed to manufacture the Grade X formulation and distribute it to each leader present today within six months. In exchange, each leader present will provide to Germany the sum of one billion dollars each. These monies will be paid in equal parts of cash and gold. Arrangements will be made to facilitate the transfer. It is agreed that production of Grade X will start within nine months. Payment to Germany from each country will be due within six months.

"Let it also be duly noted that today's meeting is significant, in that each country has agreed to bring to the table any disagreements; thereby, placing peace over war and ending any hostilities that may have been entered unto.

"Further, though this meeting is held in strict privacy, in one year, the world will be made known of this unprecedented agreement, whereby which each country will be firmly embedded with this new protocol. Gentlemen, Project Grade X will lead us into unforeseen territory. Fuhrer Hitler, you are to be applauded for development of such unchartered expertise.

"Hear ye hear ye! A toast to Adolf Hitler and his excellence." Each of the leaders raise their glass in tribute to Hitler. "And another toast to the bravery and steadfastness of each leader here today. The world will thank us for what has been accomplished here today."

"I do not believe we realize just how monumental this accord is," said Hitler through his interpreter. "Man has fought since the dawn of time. One always trying to seek the upper hand. One always choosing the conquest that leads to dominance. Man has always been peculiar, my fellow leaders. But man is awesome and resilient. I do not agree with all your respective policies and stances, yet I realize the greater picture is so much more expansive than my mind can fathom.

"Today, and for each day after, we will stand as a testament of *peace*. We will be the instruments of change that allow our people and our countries to prosper. We will have different governments with vastly different ideas, but when it comes to humanity, we will all speak the same language. I raise my glass to each of you for having the courage to do what is right."

"Cheers!" said each of the men.

"I could not have said it more poignantly," said President Roosevelt. Today is history. We are leaders of promise for all those that will come after us. The friendships created today will never falter. There are basic ideals and freedoms that we must vehemently fight for. But we will do so without the aid of force. We will do so through our strength of compassion and the elegance of our promises. Cheers!"

"You are right that our views are all different," said Stalin. "But this is no longer a game of chess. This is not strategic. It is the harmonious replication of possibilities. We represent not only what was in our old ways, but what can and will be. My comrades, I raise my glass to growth. We will grow the world together. Cheers!"

"Allow me to say thank you to my fellow leaders," said Prime Minister Konoe. "Customs and religions have been laid aside in an unprecedented determination to promote humanity over selfish idealisms. The greater of the whole picture will stand victorious and languish in peace forever more. I raise my glass in appreciation. Cheers!"

And so it happened. The leaders of the strongest countries making vows to always place humanity at the forefront of their decisions. Always allowing peace to be the underlying theme. But with humanity, man has the nasty habit of letting history repeat itself. Peace would not have the opportunity to grow old.

Chapter 12

The Setup

March 5, 1939

Adolf Hitler has a strategy meeting with one of his highest ranking officers, Heinrich Himmler. Himmler is animated and slightly paranoid in his disposition. Hitler notices right away.

"What is it that occupies your mind, Himmler?"

"My Fuhrer, it is about the pact. The pact with the other countries."

"Speak your mind then. What troubles you?"

"The Empire of Japan paid all monies due well within the allotted six-month timeframe. To date, we have received nothing from the United States or Russia."

"I am well aware of that, Himmler. I am at peace with a minor delinquency when compared to the greater good of what we accomplished."

"My Fuhrer, with all due respect, this is not the extent of what troubles me."

"Very well... proceed."

"My Fuhrer, Russia and the United States not only want sample data on Grade X, but they have also requested to send a team of their scientists to conjoin with ours. They want to see all our test data and how our scientists are running the program. Von Braun came to me this morning to speak about the request. I feel something is astray. I have a terrible pain in my gut, if I may be so bold sir."

Hitler rises and paces the floor. He is determined to not let paranoia overtake him. However, there is a familiarity that he cannot escape.

"I will admit that the two of these things together cause me some concern. These visits with our scientific team were discussed as a future option. It seems they are eager to move forward in their task. I will not allow them to circumvent our agreement. I will personally reach out to Stalin and Roosevelt. Something is awry here. You have done well, Himmler. Instruct Von Braun to redirect all requests through me for now. I will get down to the bottom of this. Leave me now."

"Yes my Fuhrer."

5 months later

The United States and Russia had not paid one penny of the agreed upon monies owed to Germany. They gave almost mirrored responses of the monies being caught up in bureaucratic red tape, always promising that the money would be transferred. Additionally, each country made repeated request for scientific technology sharing. But it wasn't these indiscretions that pushed Hitler over the tipping point.

"My Fuhrer, Mr. Kerchenkov is here." said Himmler. "Shall I show him in?"

"Yes, by all means show him in. Bring Stacks in as well, so he can act as the interpreter. And I want you to stay. This Kerchenkov visit has aroused grand interest."

Himmler leaves the office for a few moments and returns with Georgy Kerchenkov. Mr. Kerchenkov is one of Joseph Stalin's closest advisors. Hitler assured him the utmost discretion as it related to his visit.

"Fuhrer Hitler, it is a pleasure to meet you." said Mr. Kerchenkov.

"May I offer you a brandy?" Asked Hitler.

"I would be much delighted and honored. And If I may ask, may I get down to business quickly? My stay cannot extend too long or else I will open sleeping ears."

"Why yes, of course. Are you here about the money you owe us? I am getting nothing but the run around from your leader, Stalin."

"I am not here about the money, but I do know that he never had any intentions on paying you. Grade X is all he cares about. It's all that the United States cares about. President Roosevelt made a secret trip to meet with Stalin two weeks ago."

Kerchenkov's speech starts to stutter, so he quickly takes a long swallow of brandy.

"Take your time Kerchenkov. I believe you are about to tell me something of great interest."

"Fuhrer Hitler, Roosevelt and Stalin were trying to get their scientists here to steal as many secrets as possible. They wanted to learn the formulations for Grade X so they could manufacture it without you."

"Well, I have denied their scientists access, so unless I see money, and I'm reconsidering that, there will be zero sharing. They do not understand the full capabilities of Grade X. What I showed them is only a small drop in the bucket. They don't have brains on their sides with the capability to stand in the same room as my scientists… no offense, Kerchenkov."

"None taken, Fuhrer Hitler. But I must help you to see that they are no longer interested in having their scientists share intellectual processes and nomenclature. They want it all. Fuhrer, they are going to invade Germany. They mean to bring you to your knees and take the secrets for free."

"Nonsense! What are the plans? Surely the risk to do such a thing would result in a backlash from the rest of Europe, China, and Japan. Not to mention our smaller regions. How do you know your information to be 100% accurate? You've taken extreme risks to come here to share this troubling information. But still, I need something more definitive."

"Fuhrer Hitler, leaders of the United States and Russia met with French President Albert Lebrun early last month. They told him about your contempt to disavow the accord that you signed. They told him that Germany and Japan were planning an overthrow of Europe and Russia, followed by a full-on assault on American soil with Grade X technology. France now backs the US and Russia in this spurious conspiracy."

"This is nonsense. I did not disavow any agreement. There is no contempt. I *have been* the one brokering for peace. Who in the hell do Stalin and Roosevelt think they're toying with? Why not Japan? Why did they not reach out to Prime Minister Konoe?"

"They all know that Japan would support you and be against the treason the other two counties are attempting to carry out. Fuhrer Hitler, if you are to have the upper hand, you must act first."

"What is your angle in all of this, Kerchenkov? What do you plan to gain?"

"I have no angle, Fuhrer. I felt like I was about to be a part of something revolutionary. We were about to change the world and finally have a realistic shot at peace. But there is much perversion and greed. Man always seems to revert back to its natural hateful form. My principles and integrity would not allow me to stand pat while such a thing was being constructed. No good can come of this. I fear many lives may be lost. What you do with this information is now up to you, Fuhrer."

"This information has completely turned my stomach. It has shown me that Stalin and Roosevelt are nothing more than clowns, hiding behind the makeup of peacekeepers. This illustrates the desperateness of monkeys. I will take care of this.

"Kerchenkov, you have done well. I will not forget this deed. If you choose asylum, I can certainly use a man of your caliber on our team of intellectuals."

"Fuhrer, I thank you for your kind offer. I have another plan. One that might give me some finality. If I may sir, can one of your men show me to the washroom? I shall like to freshen up a bit."

"Himmler, please show our friend to my private washroom."

Himmler along with the interpreter leads Mr. Kerchenkov to Hitler's private washroom.

"Mr. Kerchenkov, I respect what you did for us." said Himmler. "Please reconsider my Fuhrer's offer. It would be great to have someone like you.

Mr. Kerchenkov smiles and closes the door behind him. Less than two minutes later there is a loud bang from a single gunshot, followed by a crashing thud noise against the door. Himmler pulls his revolver, as several soldiers rush to the area. Hitler follows suit.

"Himmler, what happened?" asked Hitler

"My Fuhrer… I believe Mr. Kerchenkov took his life."

"Open the door but be careful." Hitler draws his firearm.

As Himmler opens the door slowly, Mr. Kerchenkov's limp body falls through the opening. His revolver is still in his hand as the freshness of the single gunshot wound through his mouth gives him the finality that he sought.

"Himmler, I need you to assemble Goebells, Goering, and Speer." said Hitler. "I had hoped that the world would know us for helping to usher in a new era of peace. Now, the world will get to know us for other reasons. We will teach them to betray us."

Chapter 13

Fuhrer's Orders

August 13, 1939 Third Reich Chancellery

The Fuhrer, Adolf Hitler, walks around the table of assembled officers and looks each one of them in the eye. Today is an important meeting, as it will set into motion the beginnings of a new war.

"Before we begin with our scheduled agenda, I have some words I'd like to share with all of you. All of you are well aware of my vision for this mighty German land. You have seen the architecture so poignantly built by Speer. You have heard the voices of the German people demanding it.

"What many of you don't know is that I attempted to share this vision with our partners in other countries. Namely, the US, Russia, and Japan. The leaders of these three countries and myself met in France last September to sign into existence the greatest peace agreement ever known to man.

"While each country shared different beliefs and customs, it was agreed that we would always come to the table with peaceful solutions to any issues. For the first time, military action and other forms of violence would no longer be used to bargain for position. But sadly, that historic day is now just that, a part of history. Japan has proven to be our only true friend. The US and Russia have proven to be lecherous bigots. They are attempting to undermine all that we know to be dear and true. They will stop at nothing to pillage our knowledge.

"Today gentlemen we assemble to discuss our vision once again. But this time, we are forging ahead with speed and vengeance. The US and Russia will pay. The mighty will fall with haste. We will dispose of them just like we will dispose of the first topic on our agenda. Both of these tasks will be handled simultaneously. Further discussion will be granted in a few days. But for now, we have some other business to take care of. Himmler, please read the first topic on the agenda."

"Yes my Fuhrer. The first topic deals with *The Question*."

"And what is that question, Himmler?"

Himmler looks around the table at the other officers before speaking.

"The question is what to do with the population of over 11 million Jews."

Hitler stops his stroll around the table for a quick pause and then continues to circle it.

"Do you have the breakdown of Jews by area as instructed?"

"Yes, my Fuhrer, I have copies, enough to share with everyone here."

"Then pass them out and take notice. This is no longer a question. The solution is quite simple. The Jewish people are dirty and cast a shadow of grotesqueness throughout

Europe. They all must be annihilated. Every one of them. Every man, woman, and child. Himmler, I want your efforts stepped up in the creation of the camps we've been discussing. The purge starts right away."

Himmler smiles delightfully, as if he was just given a new toy.

"Right away, my Fuhrer. I will assemble the rest of the teams tomorrow."

"Very good. Now, tell me about the second item on the agenda."

"It involves Poland... the correction of Poland."

"Correction indeed." said Hitler as he finally makes his way to his seat at the head of the table. "Gentlemen, the world shall witness our glory. The opposed shall taste the leather on our boots. We invade Poland on Sept 1st, which is exactly one year after that shit agreement I signed my name to. Once we crush Poland, we will do the same to the red dogs of Russia, and then on to our bigoted friends in the United States."

Hitler rises and moves to the far table where he rolls over a cart filled with glasses and bottles of whisky. He places a glass in front of each of his officers and fills them with imported whiskey.

"Raise your glasses high, gentlemen. This is the start of many celebrations such as this. We shall conquer the world."

"Heil Hitler, Heil Hitler, Heil Hitler." are the chants in unison from his officers. The dice have been rolled.

Chapter 14

One Last Drink

April 27, 1945

Nearly six years after Hitler met with his principle officers to discuss the initial strategies of WWII, Germany is reeling after several military defeats. Their military is decimated, but their leader is completely rejuvenated.

"What is lost is not everything." said Hitler. "What is lost does not predispose us to failure. Our lives and our ideals have been forever sealed in blood. The stench of radical misnomers run rampant. They dare to cross our lines and make a spectacle of what they are trying to protect.

"They are not here to end anything. They are here to form a new beginning. A new beginning without me. A new beginning based on incredulous greed. They call me an animal. They call our party treacherous. But only the well informed few know the true intentions of their debauchery.

"Mark my words when I tell you that this is not the end. The weak will continue to be just that. We shall rise again, and we will be more powerful than any man can fathom. The world will kneel at our feet. Do you have complete confidence that all preparations have been soundly met?"

"Yes, my Fuhrer." said Albert Speer. "Everything is just as you instructed. If I must say so, it's happening just as you laid out. This is pure genius."

"When you lay a big trap, you need an even bigger piece of cheese. The genius is in your design, my dear friend. Your loyalty will be rewarded. Your personal sacrifices will not be left in vain. We haven't long now. They will be here in a matter of days. Those arrogant dogs. Come, one final drink, and then Ava can finally have peace. Heil victory, Speer."

"Heil victory, my Fuhrer."

Chapter 15

B rooke continues to listen to Mr. Trekker, as she has a familiar numb feeling overtaking her. She makes comparisons between Hitler and Bartholomew Gainsborough.

"The bad guys were good, but we made them bad."

"I'm sorry Brooke, I don't follow you."

"No, Mr. Trekker, I apologize. It's just this information you've given me is a total contradiction to everything. I'm just dumbfounded why I'm the one to be having this extraordinary information shared with. So, what about the concentration camps and everything else that happened? Surely that wasn't a ruse? I mean you were there."

"Not at all. After Kerchenkov committed suicide, Hitler met with his top advisors. They came up with a plan to cripple the US, Russia, and the rest of Europe. The rest of what you know about history is correct... well with one exception."

"Oh boy. OK, what's the exception?"

"The exception is where we ran cold. Here, I want to show you something."

Mr. Trekker places a leather satchel on the counter and takes out a bundle of folded pieces of paper, all wound tightly with rubber bands, along with a stray journal.

"This is another relic from that horrible dark time. These are letters from many of those that died at the concentration camp. These letters were written to their loved ones in the event they were able to survive the menace. All of these are enormously heartbreaking to read. And this journal on top is from Hans himself. On his second and last visit to Auschwitz, he gave me this. Due to its small size, it was quite easy to conceal. He told me if I died, this journal went with me. And If I lived, we had plenty to discuss if we were also both fortunate to survive the war."

"What kind of journal is it?"

Mr. Trekker removes the rubber band.

"Here, I want you to read it. You are the only other person that this has been shared with. I realize all of this information is a severe overload, but I promise to make sense of all of this for you."

Brooke carefully opens the journal, admiring the antique musk brimming through the pages.

January 17, 1944

Operation trading places has been implemented. Eva Braun is dead. Her fever could not be controlled. I saw her replacement. She looks just like her. Her name is Reina from the US. Albert Speer has worked it out?

January 20, 1944

There is someone new. He is not a soldier, but the Fuhrer is spending lots of time one on one with him.

The Fuhrer won't listen to any of us. This plan will not work. Himmler agrees with me. We will all die trying to chase this fascination.

"Who wrote this Mr. Trekker?"

"Goebells wrote this. It was his personal journal. Hans was in the right place at the right time when Goebells dropped it in the field. Goebells was paranoid when he couldn't find it; nonetheless, he was a smart man. He never placed his name anywhere in the journal, and he wrote it with his left hand… of course he was right-handed."

"So, Eva Braun didn't die alongside Hitler in 1945?"

"No Brooke, Eva's body was found in the same way it had been reported. But Eva had already long been dead. They found a stand-in for her. But Why? That is where we draw a cold lead. Hitler created something called Operation Trading Places, but Han's and I have no idea what that meant. We believe it has something to do with this person named Reina.

"Brooke, this all happened so long ago, do you have any connections that might be able to trace this person? Perhaps through her we will find those long elusive answers. Even if she no longer lives, she may have left something behind that will aide us. Her story must be tied to the ugly bombs somehow. Please help us to understand why."

"Mr. Trekker, I will do what I can to assist you, but I have to be completely honest with you. All my time and resources are going into preparation for this presidential debate. I will place some calls for you; however, this is not something I can become fully engaged in at this point."

"I appreciate your straightforwardness, Brooke. I don't know how time sensitive this whole issue is. But its importance should not be relegated. Any help you can provide would be critical to this matter. I am an old man now with limited resources. I would be made a fool of talking about any of this information outside of you. Even you must tread lightly. But your resources are certainly vaster than mine. Together, we might be able to figure this complicated story out."

"There is one thing you can give me some clarity on. What is Grade X?"

"I told you I was an old man." Mr. Trekker said, as he sits back in his chair. "Grade X is still some of the finest technology out there."

Chapter 16

Grade X and the Super Soldier

H ans learned a great deal from Albert Speer," said Mr. Trekker. Speer was an architectural wizard, and Hitler's closest friend. Hans reminded Speer of his own young son and took to him quickly. Hans was also an engineering student and could speak certain jargon and read blueprints, which highly appealed to him.

"Speer at some point thought that Germany would be successful in defeating all of Europe. He began plans on the next phases of the operation. An operation that would require a man of Han's caliber and intellect. Speer had begun work on a full-scale model of what New Germany would look like. Ironically, it was one of the few things that were left unblemished by the massive bombing campaigns. Speer shared with Hans many of the details of Grade X technology and how they would use it. If the Grade X deployment would have been successful, we would have had a very different Germany, and of course a much different world.

"To say that Hitler had the top scientists in the world on his team would be a gross understatement. The theories and applied sciences that his team used placed them many years in advance of anything anyone else was doing in the world. The United States, Russia, and Japan had an inkling of this information. However, none of them knew just how technologically and scientifically savvy Hitler and his team were. Now, I won't go too far in the weeds with a scientific explanation, but Hitler's team went a step beyond plutonium-239 and uranium-238 that's been used for bomb production.

"They were able to produce uranium with ease. This was something that made the United States very nervous. The scientists found a way to use a binder of a new chemical that they created called rexonium. They conducted experiments binding plutonium with rexonium. The binder increased plutonium's destructive mass by well over 1000%. One bomb, the size of a motorcycle could take out an entire city like New York in less than half an hour with ground impact. If I can put this advancement of technology into perspective Brooke, this is something no one is able to duplicate to this very day."

Brooke is engaged but perplexed. "So, the technology and the knowhow were lost?"

"Well yes and no. I'm going to get to that in just a few moments."

"My apologies for interrupting you. I am completely bewildered yet fascinated by this information. Please continue."

"Yes, indeed. Somehow Russia gained intel on the research the German's were conducting. Mind you this intel was limited. There was even talk that Hitler's research progress was purposely leaked to evidence his superiority and might. Regardless, of how the information got into

Russia's hands, Stalin started his rapid instigation. He warned Roosevelt of what could be accomplished if Hitler were allowed to advance his military. The weapons and the science behind the weapons were not something either country could touch. Mind you, Hitler was going to willingly share much of his research with all three countries. There was simply no need for the egregious actions of Russia and the United States. I suppose Hitler knew better and kept some key elements of his research close to the vest. That was one of the primary reasons he wouldn't allow the other countries to send in their scientists. Paranoia has its advantages.

"Stalin and Roosevelt attempted to liaise with Japan; however, Prime Minister Konoe refused to assist with what he called treachery. He accused Russia and the United States of *malicious bullying*. Stalin considered Japan a bench player at most. Had it not been for their scientific and engineering prowess, surely China would have been a much better partner. But this did not sit well with Roosevelt at all. So much so, by the end of WWII, the United States dropped two atomic bombs on them. But once again, I'm going way off course. These conversations always get my blood boiling, Brooke. It's yet another illustration of how greed rules man. As you can see, smoke and mirrors are quite prevalent in this story.

"Would you like to take a break, Mr. Trekker?"

"No, not at all. I must finish at least these details, but thank you kindly. So, where was I? Yes, Grade X had a duality, Brooke. The German scientists used rexonium as a binder to create much more destructive bombs. But guess what? It was used for something else even more remarkable. Please excuse my poor choice of words, but I must admit it was indeed remarkable. Do you know the story behind the Nazi SS?"

"I want to say I do, Mr. Trekker; however, I'm thinking you're going to completely mitigate anything I've learned. So, I will say very little."

Mr. Trekker smiles.

"The SS was founded in 1925. The *Schutzstaffel*, for what it was originally named, is German for Protective Echelon. They initially served as Hitler's personal bodyguards, and later became one of the most powerful and feared organizations in all of Nazi Germany."

"OK, so that much I did know. But here comes the curve ball, right?"

"Precisely. The SS was also known within the ranks of Hitler's scientists and top officers as *Super Soldier*. The scientists found a way to infuse rexonium into the musculoskeletal system. The results were astounding. It embedded itself deep within the muscle tissues and the central nervous system. They used one test subject for their research. The test subject was as strong as a silver back gorilla, with supreme agility and quickness. And get this, no side effects. But that wasn't the most remarkable thing, Brooke. The test subject was immune to high doses of radioactivity. He could drink a cocktail of plutonium, uranium and rexonium without blinking an eye.

"Can you imagine what the world would be like today had we continued to broker peace with Germany and the rest of the world? I challenge that history would not be the same, Brooke. There may never have been a holocaust. There may never had been atomic bombs dropped. Perhaps all those millions of lives lost would have been responsible for helping us to usher in a new day and age. But man is… man. And this is the result of everything."

"The test subject… What happened to him, Mr. Trekker? Were there more of them?"

"There was only one subject. Hans met him on one occasion in the lab. His name was Heinz Gruber. He was a 16-year-old boy. The plan was to continue testing for at least a year before making any additional determinations. Due to hostilities quickly escalating, the project was placed on hold, only to never be revisited. No one had ever heard from or saw him again. But here, take a look at these. These are some group pictures of Hitler, his top officers, and scientists. And the one seated in front of them all is Heinz Gruber. The next picture gives a much better close-up of his face.

"Hitler became paranoid with his test data going into the wrong hands. Heinz disappeared, and then the Fuhrer had several of his scientists committed to Auschwitz for conspiracy. Everything else happened as you know it in the history books. Hitler invaded Poland, and all hell broke loose afterwards. Japan's continued misalignment with the United States prompted the big drop… twice. And now we are back in a familiar place. On the brink of war. And our trail runs cold here.

"Something is not right about this whole situation. I can feel it deeply and firmly. Brooke, we need your help. We need your resources. We need God right now more than ever. Can you please help us?"

"I don't know what to say, Mr. Trekker. Sure, I will do whatever I can to help. Can I take these pictures with me? I might have someone in the federal bracket that could lend some assistance."

"Yes, you may take them. I'm sure you will take extra good care of them. Please keep in touch and let me know what you were able to find. And if you need more of a hidden history lesson, please call on me.

"Will do, Mr. Trekker. I promise to give this a full-court press. But first, I have to finish my preparation for this presidential debate."

"Good luck to you Brooke. The world will know your name and smile one day soon."

Chapter 17

Debate Chatter

September 26, 2016 1st Presidential Debate

Wright State University and city of Dayton are buzzing with anticipation for tonight's first presidential debate between Democrat Barbara Spelling and Independent, and poll leader, Simon *Sim* City. After months of preparation, mentoring, and coaching Brooke is ready for the biggest moment of her professional career. She and Charlie take a break from the frenzy and enjoy some quiet time.

"So, how are feeling, Miss Moderator?" asked Charlie. "I'm sure this has to be the most action Dayton has ever seen. It's bananas here."

"I know. I feel like this part of Ohio might collapse from all of the people here." Brooke said as she smiles. "I know I'm ready, Charlie, but there's still this sense of nervousness that will probably never go away. I'm sure it will be heightened this evening. If you think about all the stories we've covered together, not including of the Milk and Thaddeus, they were in our local markets of St. Petersburg and now Detroit. Depending on what we were covering, we might have had a few thousand people see our telecast. And, even if we were lucky to have more, there was this down-home feeling to it all. We didn't personally know most of the people that surrounded us, but that didn't eliminate the strong sense of family. Do you know what I mean?"

"Yeah, I get it. Regardless of what we covered, it was like we were doing it for this small and close-knit group. Those people in our markets are our extended family."

"Absolutely. And here we are in a place where there won't be thousands, there will be millions of people watching this debate from all over the world. Charlie, Sim City is not just a presidential candidate, he's a friggin rock star. When in the history of politics, have we seen such a landslide in poll numbers? This is like *Presidential Woodstock*. The people's voice is loud, clear and unanimous."

"Yes, it is, Brooke. And an extreme high five for landing the post interview with both candidates. You are on fire. I am so proud of you partner. You deserve all the success that's coming your way. You wear it well."

They exchange their signature high five as Brooke rises and looks out the window of the dean's office that has been their sanctuary since they arrived.

"You know what makes this day the most special, Charlie? Having my mom and dad here. I'm so glad they could make it, especially my dad. This trip is more challenging for him than he'd let anyone know. But, at the same time, I know there's no place he'd rather be. I am truly blessed."

"I couldn't have said it better. Your parents are right where they want to and *need to* be. OK, Miss Moderator, it's time to go mix and mingle. Let's see what type of lunch they have prepared for us. And be nice to any CNN people you might be sitting next to."

He gives her the concerned dad face before breaking into a smile.

"Really, Charlie? You know me… look at this smile. I'm always nice. There is no competition, only news. I'm ready to do this."

"You and I know that, but someone needs to tell them that. Let's go eat!"

9pm the debate begins

Tonight's debate has made history in so many ways. The viewership for this debate has broken all previous records for any type of telecast. It is the first in which a female candidate represents a major political party, but by far the buzz is all about the independent candidate, Simon City, who leads in every poll in every state in high double-digit numbers. These debates seem to be nothing more than a formality for the obvious choice for the 45th president of the United States.

The college is jammed tight with thousands in attendance. In an unprecedented move, the campus has special giant screens in the center of the campus and the parking lots to show the live feed of the debate. There are easily well over 5000 onlookers outside of the event. The college campus has been turned into an oversized tailgating party. There is a literal sea of posters touting their approval for Simon City.

Half-way through the debate and the ratings are through the roof. The strength and wisdom of selecting Brooke to moderate has been met with exceptional success. She has not only upped the air of credibility, but she has also done an incredible job of mixing up the questions and themes to truly showcase and mirror those things that matter most to the voters. Also, her eloquence has allowed each candidate an opportunity to be at the very top of their respective game. She even found a way to lighten it up with some humorous jabs at each candidate. This debate will surely set the bar for all those that follow.

"Mr. City, I'd like to ask you the same question." said Brooke. "*Black Lives Matter* is now a huge movement. Has our country gone in reverse as it relates to race relations? If chosen as president, what would your administration do to address this?"

"Thank you, Miss Hannah. Everyone knows me well enough to know I'm going to tell it like it is. I want to point out that I agree with my fellow candidate, Mrs. Spelling when she said, *all lives matter.* I could not have stated that more poignantly. But I want to discuss black lives for a moment. For more than three hundred years, these lives only mattered as property or labor. Imagine being treated like you were lower than a dog and being brainwashed as such. We're talking generations of families. Grandparents and great grandparents, fathers, mothers, daughters, and sons. Everyone growing up and growing old knowing their lives… their own existence meant nothing in the eyes of so many. When you are brainwashed for that long, for so many centuries, it doesn't just affect Black lives anymore. That type of inhumane indecency affects us all. We psychologically, whether willing or unwilling, embedded our minds with the premise that Black lives were not the same as everyone else's. While us here in the United States worked on reprogramming our minds to acknowledge and accept, the minds of many Blacks had to be reprogrammed so that they could acknowledge that they belonged.

"I realize that I will face backlash for what I'm about to say, but our society has acted too damn slow to prove these lives have always mattered, and they were always equal, and that there is no color… only clarity."

The crowd both indoors and out erupt into a thunderous applause and standing ovation. Even candidate Spelling turns and offers her admiration of his comments.

"Thank you- -- thank you." said Mr. City. "I'm not going to stand here and tell you that there will be more programs implemented, and that if I'm elected, that my administration will bring us closer together. First off, there are already too many programs in place that aren't effective. Some aren't effective because they haven't been devoted the resources that are needed to make such a thing happen. While some others are unsuccessful because they just aren't needed. As your president, I will work to ensure that we have the right programs in place, and that they are utilized to the utmost of their abilities. I'm also not going to stand here and tell you that my administration will end racism as we know it.

"There are no programs, no amount of money, and no amount of protests that will change the mentality of some. There are some that just don't care, and nothing will change that. For some... key word *some*, it's a lifestyle decision. They are well aware of their choices and are fluent in their thoughts. No president, and no administration can change these people.

"In that regard, racism *may* always be with us, because some look at it as an acceptable difference. Much like deciding which pair of pants to wear. But these people are the minority. These people are the dying breed. These people will not build our foundation. We will build our foundation over theirs. They will be left behind. They won't matter *until we all matter*."

The crowd goes nuts. Chants of *Sim City* can be heard at a deafening pitch. Mr. City receives a standing ovation for nearly five minutes. The debate ends with as much buzz as it began with. The early editions of the newspapers are almost ready to go to print, and world is almost settled back down. But first, they await Brooke's one on one post interview with the candidates.

Chapter 18

After five minutes of prep time, both candidates are eager for one last audience with the voters through this one on one interview with Brooke. With so many viewers staying glued to their televisions, this marks the optimal time to sway some stragglers.

"Mrs. Spelling, this campaign, your campaign is special for so many reasons." said Brooke. "You were the clear and unanimous favorite for the Democratic Party. At one point you were the clear front runner for the White House. And now we have Independent candidate, Simon City with double digit leads in every single state, including your own. What happened? What are you going to do to turn this ship around?

"Well, Brooke, it's simple. I just didn't keep the intensity of my Democratic nomination. I let off the accelerator a bit, while my counterpart nailed it to the floor. But rest assured, my tank is full, my convictions are strong, and I am pedal to the floor from here on out. I must also give credit where it is due. Mr. City has run a very smart campaign. He's been able to resonate with many. But just as you stated, there are so many things that make this election special for me. I'm going to utilize those things to showcase why I'm the obvious choice for the people."

"OK, here's the tough question. If you were not the nominee, would you support Mr. City as president? He has quite the agenda for bringing all political parties together, especially the Republicans and Democrats."

"I am a servant to the people, Brooke. If they spoke and chose Mr. City as their president, I would do my very best to ensure our country and our liberties are upheld to the highest standards."

"So, I can take that as a yes, Mrs. Spelling?"

"You may take that as a yes."

"Mrs. Spelling, it's been great having such a personal one on one chat with you. Thank you for taking the time to sit with me and the WDIV Channel 4 news team. Best of luck to you for the remainder of your campaign."

"Thank you for having me, Brooke. I'm available to speak with you anytime."

"Up next our one-on-one conversation continues with presidential front-runner Simon City."

Mr. Simon City was given the nickname *Sim City* by one of his staffers, being named after a popular video game. Mr. City has the Hollywood good looks of Clark Gable with deep blue eyes. He is well fit and tall with charisma and charm that is simply unforgettable. For as much of his life that's public, there are still many details that he has been able to keep private.

"Alright, Brooke, we have three minutes before Mr. Sim city makes his entrance." said Charlie. "You did another awesome job. Looks like you're buying the next round of iced coffees."

"HEY… well whatever you say, bud. One more then we are home free, and I get to take these darn stockings off and relax.

"OK, heads up, he's coming in.

"Miss Brooke Hannah, what an awesome job back there." said Mr. City. "Are you sure you can't moderate the remainder of these?"

"You're far to kind, Mr. City, please take a seat and."

Charlie gives the countdown. "And we're live in five, four, three, two, one …"

"Welcome back to WDIV Channel 4's special post coverage of the 2016 Presidential Debate. Joining us live is the front runner, Mr. Simon City. Mr. City welcome. And, on behalf of the station, please allow me to thank you for spending a few moments with us."

"Thank you for having me, Brooke. It's a pleasure to be here. I suppose we have both hit a milestone today. We both have a presidential debate under our belts.

"That's right. We sure do, and what a wonderful segue into my first question. Early reports are showing this debate to be the most watched event in television history. The surroundings here at Wright State University look more like a super bowl celebration than a debate amongst politicians. Tell us how you think you did tonight, and why all the buzz surrounding this particular presidential campaign?"

"I believe I did well tonight, Brooke. And once again I must tip my hat to you for orchestrating a great debate. You allowed both of us to give it everything we had. I don't feel like there was a miss on the important items I wanted to discuss. I also must agree that this is unlike anything I've ever experienced. This atmosphere has been electrifying and magical all-day long.

"You want to know what the appeal is? Well, Brooke, I believe it's a few different things, and I'm going to have to speak it like it is if you don't mind."

"Your brutal honesty has resonated with the people throughout your campaign, so I implore you to continue to the same."

"Thank you, Brooke. In many ways I can draw parallels to our current president, which leads me to the first reason. I am vastly different than any of the other choices the people had the opportunity to choose from. I represent change on a much higher plateau. President Lewis is the first black president in the history of the US. His nomination marked a huge shift in the political landscape. Our country was ready for a change, and so they elected him not once but twice. And now the country is ready for another change. They are looking for something different. This is what they believe they've found in me. And while these differences represent the sentiment of the majority of my followers, there are a small number of those that fall underneath another umbrella... entertainment and bias.

"I realize this next statement might sound raw; however, I believe it to be true. Again, I want to paint another parallel with President Lewis. There is a subset of voters that elected him just because his is black. They didn't care about his foreign policy agenda, his stance against terror, or what his 4-year plan might have been. They felt allegiance to ensure something magical happened that for generations was never thought possible. I have resonated with a subset of the voters because of my resemblance to an old Hollywood star. I'm also a fireball and people are entertained by my banter.

"But the reason President Lewis has served two terms, and I'm ahead in the polls is because the people know deep down that we could make a difference. I'm gonna make the world explode one day. Explode with something that has been sorely lacking… humanity. And my final point or reason that people are more engaged with me comes to this. People are sick and tired of politicians pointing the finger. No party can ever do it right or take credit for anything, because the other parties will always find fault. And, by the way, the President is not responsible for everything that goes wrong in this country and in our own households. I'm all about accountability and credibility.

"Look at the polls for other races around the country recently. The voices of the people have been heard loud and clear. Enough is enough. As political leaders, we must band together for everything we attest to holding sacred. If this country is to ever be as great as it can be, we must embrace that *United* word we seem to take for granted. If I'm elected, I will unite us all under one common and boisterous theme… *Together we shall achieve.*"

"Those are powerful words indeed, Mr. City, and together we shall achieve has been consistent throughout your campaign. So, we're almost out of time, but as a local Detroit girl I have to ask you a question, being that you are a tremendous football fan. Can I get the Lions in the Super bowl for 2017?"

"Hmmm. Well Brooke, I think you should just focus on moderating for right now. Your Tiger's look good though." he said as they both laugh.

"Mr. City, thank you again for joining us and best of luck to you in the race for the White House."

"Thank you for having me, Brooke. Awesome job and best wishes to you. I'm sure we'll rub elbows again."

"On behalf of the news team at WDIV, I'd like to thank you all for joining us. I'm Brooke Hannah... Goodnight!"

As Brooke has a brief off-camera conversation with Mr. City and Charlie, the small town of Dayton Ohio and the country is abuzz at the conclusion of the debates and one on one interviews. Brooke's phone has been lighting up like a Christmas tree with calls and text messages of encouragement and praise. Her station manager, Birdy Coswell gave her the next couple of days off to deconstruct and revel in the wonderful job she did. There are two VIP's that occupy her thoughts and anxiously await her. She excuses herself and makes a bee line to the floor.

"Mom --- dad! Did you have a good time? How did I do? Dad, are you feeling, OK? Was it a mistake not to wear any make-up? What about my..."

"Calm down, Brooke, my goodness." said her mother as all three of them embrace tightly. "Everything was wonderful. You are wonderful. Oh my, how proud I am right now."

"No tears mom, I don't wanna cry tonight."

"Look at my baby girl." said her dad. "I was listening to you in awe. I thought about that night I was telling you bedtime stories, and you had a million and one questions. I remember telling you that you were the most beautiful princess ever, and that another one there would never be. You are so much like your mother. So much poise and grace. So much dignity. They are eating you up just like I knew they would. But you know what makes this whole thing, your whole journey even more special for me? You never stopped being Brooke. You are your own woman playing by your own rules. I'm --- I." He is unsuccessful at stopping the flowing tears.

"Thanks a lot dad, now we're all a mess."

They all embrace and take in every strand of the evening for everything its worth. Tonight, has affirmed it... Brooke Hannah has arrived.

Chapter 19

Taking the First Step

Two days later

Brooke takes her time off in stride. She uses it to catch up on some lost commitments with friends and enjoys some quality time with her parents. Mr. Trekker has been occupying her mind. With the debate out of the way, she can now wrap her mind around what she might be able to do to assist, but first her cell phone suddenly rings.

"Hello, this is Brooke. wait a minute. Detective Engler?"

"Brooke. Hello there. Yes, it's me. It's good to hear your voice. Since you're a big-time star now, I thought you may have forgotten about the little guys."

"Ha ha, detective. Oh, my goodness, it's so good to hear from you too. What's going on with you? Wait, is everything OK?"

"Yes, everything is going well. Chief Jared is still raising hell around here like usual. We had a few guys retire, but we had a really good recruiting class. One of the best I've seen in years. We are at full capacity now. So, listen. The reason I was calling you was to let you know I'm coming to Michigan in December. There's a huge law enforcement conference on the 15th, and I was wondering since I'm going to be in Detroit anyway… If you'd like to, I dunno, grab some dinner or something like that?"

"Detective Engler, are you asking me out on a date?" said Brooke with a stern but joking voice.

"Well, no, it's nothing like that, Brooke. I was just… well you know… Yeah, I figured it would be nice to see you. I'm really bad at this."

"It would be great to see you too, detective. Let's stay in touch and make some firm arrangements closer to that time. I'm looking forward to it."

"So yes? You'll go? I mean thank you, Brooke. Great! OK I will call you soon. This made my day. Gotta go now. Please take care."

"You as well detective." she said as she hangs up the phone laughing hysterically. "You're a cutie… why not!?"

Brooke goes through her favorite contacts on her phone and dials her good friend and FBI Agent, Lana Quivner.

"Well, well, well. Hello, Miss International News. Thank you for finally returning my phone call. How are you doing? Girl you killed it on Monday night. Your name and Simon City's is all over the internet and the news. You need to check your Twitter account sometimes."

"Thank you, Lana. I'm sorry I took so long to call you back. And thank you for watching and giving your support and prayers. I definitely needed all of them. Heck still do. Listen, I need a favor, and this one is strange."

"Oh boy, here we go. Is this something that teeters right there on the edge of what I can and can't do?"

"The truth is I'm really not sure. How far back do your records go? Can you research something back from the WWII era?"

"Umm sure. We have archived data of many records and events. What is it you are looking for? And yeah, this sounds quite interesting… WWII?"

"I might have a story. I'm not sure at this point. I need to put together some variables to get a clearer picture."

"OK. What information do you need?"

"I have two names. The first is a girl. Her name is Reina. She was a US citizen. At some point she either moved to or temporarily stayed in Germany. The second person's name is Heinz Gruber. More than likely, that is no longer his name, but it's all that I have for right now. If this is toeing the line in anyway, please tell me so. I don't want to jeopardize your job over this."

"Not to worry, girlie. You're just asking about names right now, so let's just start there. This is going to take me some time to put together. Can I call you back in a couple of days or so?"

"Yes, no rush. Get back to me whenever you can. I truly appreciate this."

"I know you do, and don't worry, I will let you owe me one gladly."

Alright, the ball is in motion. Brooke dials Mr. Trekker.

"Brooke, it's really good to hear from you. Of course, I, like the whole world it seems watched the presidential debate. You handled yourself like a well-oiled pro. I'm very proud of you, young lady. I know your grandfather would have been even prouder. I didn't expect a call from you so soon. Do you have news already?"

"Hello, Mr. Trekker. Thank you so much for watching and supporting me. I wish my grandfather could have been there to see it too. But having mom and dad there really made it special for me. I don't have any news yet. I'm calling to let you know that I have reached out to one of my contacts to give us a hand with this. And don't worry, this is being handled with anonymity and the utmost privacy."

"I had zero worries this information was being given the level of attention it needed. I worry Brooke. I wish I had the opportunity to speak with Hans before he passed away. He gave you that information, as something must have happened. Something changed. While I appreciate everything you are doing, I ask that you proceed cautiously. We aren't discussing meager classroom politics. Is there anything else I can offer you?"

"Not at this time, Mr. Trekker. I will await the results from my contact and follow up with you thereafter."

"Thank you, Brooke. I look forward to hearing from you soon."

Three weeks later

"Hello, this is Brooke!"

"Hey, girlie, it's Lana. I'm calling from my work cell. You got a minute?"

"Yes, give me just a moment." Brooke said as she walks away from her desk at the news station. "OK, how's it going, missy? Is this about that info?"

"Yes, it is. So, first off, I'm still working on this. The information you gave was minimal, but I've been able to find out some interesting stuff so far. I believe I found your Reina, and if it's the right person, she also had a twin brother. I haven't had time to finish the necessary cross referencing, and I must be honest with you in saying I'm going to have to put the brakes on this one till sometime after the first of the year. There's so much going on right now, not to mention the heightened level of security for the presidential election and subsequent inauguration. Is that going to be alright?"

"Yes, Lana, absolutely. So, twins huh? Sounds quite interesting. The plot thickens."

"I have no idea what you are working on, but I hope whatever it is, it doesn't end up like that psycho mess you got roped into."

Brooke pulls the phone away from her ear staring at it briefly. She knows she's being *roped in* again. And like last time, she has no idea what she's getting herself involved with.

"Well, that makes two of us. I believe this is just another story that might possibly be able to go on a front page. There's a lot going on, I get it. Let's circle back up after the holidays. If anything changes before then, please buzz me."

"You got it. I'll be checking in on you beforehand anyway. We need to discuss another getaway."

"Thank you, Lana, I look forward to it."

Brooke decides to wait sharing the new development with Mr. Trekker until it can be fully validated.

The upcoming months proved to be almost just as busy between the candidates swinging in and out of town, and her workload increasing with one of her colleagues on leave.

Chapter 20

Presidential Record

November 8, 2016

The presidential election had been concluded and in no surprise to anyone, Simon City is easily elected as the 45th President of the United States breaking the record set in 1984 by Ronald Daly. The president elect chooses to have his acceptance speech on the floor of the place where his father took him when he was a little boy, Madison Square Gardens. The arena is filled to capacity, while thousands of others are implanted just outside as he gives his speech. Brooke, Charlie, and several other colleagues from WDIV are in attendance at courtside for the most celebrated event in recent history.

"I dunno, Brooke, I think City should have been a coach." said Charlie as he almost has to yell into Brooke's ear due to the volume of elation in the arena. "Can you imagine what kind of team we might have back in Detroit with him at the helm? This guy can motivate the pants off a fly."

Brooke returning the same equally matched volume. "Yeah, I agree with you, he would have been an awesome coach. He will get all the practice he needs dealing with the Senate and the House."

The arena suddenly grows louder as everyone rises in standing ovation as President Elect Simon City and Vice President Laura Saulters makes their transition to center court. It takes several minutes to quiet the crowd down so he can speak. He is overwhelmed by the support.

"Thank you… thank you all from the bottom of our hearts. Team City is here. We made it!"

The crowd erupts into another round of loud cheers and chants of Sim City. After another moment, he begins again.

"Tonight, is not about Simon City or Laura Saulters. It's not about polls, elections, or final tallies. Tonight, is not about the darkness that continues to try to fade the light. No, it's much deeper than that. It's more emotional than that. It's more personal than that. We are here because we have unanimously agreed that moving forward from reverse is the only direction we shall *traverse*. We are here because nothing can or will happen without unyielding and unabashed support. We are here because beyond a shadow of a doubt, we know we have the power to make a difference.

"We are in the valley of that which we continue to be ignorant to. Some of our allies are *moving* in an opposite course. We are fighting one of our greatest enemies as they continue to infiltrate and poison innocent minds. Our gentle Mother Earth is slowly dying. These are all real issues that we must address right now. We began this journey just over a year ago when all of you… all of us said, *we could*. Laura and I are here tonight to represent with every breath and every molecule in our bodies that, *we will*. Now enough talk, time for action. Let us celebrate our new world tonight. Let us start building it tomorrow."

Confetti flies and fills the positive cadence of the arena air. Everyone is on their feet as the local high school band plays their hearts out. Outside the arena is another amalgamation of hope, tears, and relentless spirits embracing this historic event. Hours later, in the wee hours of the morning, Brooke and Charlie are still wired. They sit and continue to converse in the lobby of the hotel after the rest of their colleagues decide to call it a night.

"Well, Charlie, I have to say I am thoroughly impressed. That was the shortest acceptance speech ever. But you know what, it was perfect. It matched everything Simon City has been about since he jumped on the scene just over a year ago. Adding Laura Saulters as his running mate, and soon to be vice president shows tremendous foresight and courage. I have a good feeling about this president. I believe he will be able to unite us all."

"I have to admit I wasn't impressed at first, despite adding Saulters to the ticket, I thought he was going to be another suit and tie that would try to sway voters with his looks and charm. But he has been the complete opposite. He has won everyone over, including me, with his strong sense of humanism and cooperative spirit. He was masterful during each debate, and he hasn't changed his stance on anything he said he believed in from early on. Politicians always shift... so far, he hasn't. I'm a fan. Let's see what he can do. I intend to do my part."

"Well, he is a charmer for sure. The easy on the eye thing doesn't do him any harm whatsoever, Charlie... I'm just saying. I have a feeling he is just getting started. Something tells me he will prove to be quite interesting, which is probably hugely understated."

President Simon City is sworn into office as the 45th President of the United States on January 20, 2017. He and the vice president go to work quickly with members of congress. The passion of unity spreads far and wide. President City proves quickly that he is much different than any of his predecessors.

Chapter 21

Two Glasses Please

December 15, 2016 4:45pm

J ust as Brooke gets into her car, her phone vibrates and the picture id displays a face that always makes her smile.

"Hello dad. How are you doing?"

"Hello honey, I am doing good. Did I catch you at a bad time? I wasn't quite sure if you were off work yet."

"Yes, I am off, and anytime is a good time, Mr. Dad. So whatcha up to?"

"Well, nothing right now, but listen can you keep a secret?"

"Here we go! What are you trying to hide from mom now?

"WHAT!? I don't hide things from your mother. It's just, you know, she doesn't always agree on my direction."

"And, sometimes, I don't either. What have you done, dad?"

"Well, let me give you some good news. My blood pressure and cholesterol have stabilized and have been at normal levels for some time now. So much so, the doctor is giving me lower dosages of meds for both. He said if I keep it up, I might be able to get off both of them in the next 60 days."

"DAD! That's awesome. I am so proud of you. You have been working extra hard with your diet and it's paying off."

"I don't plan on going anywhere for a very long time. I still have plenty that I need to do."

"You are absolutely right. You won't be going anywhere for a very long time. Now, tell me what you did?"

"So, I had your mother run some errands for me, as well as her having to do some of her own. I knew she would be gone for a while. As soon as the coast was clear, I called Happy's Pizza and had them deliver some fries with a side of barbeque sauce. My order didn't meet the minimum for delivery, but I really didn't care what they were going to charge me.

"When they got there, I went outside and ate every single one of them. I threw away the garbage in Mrs. Green's garbage can and none knew the wiser. And before you yell at me, the doctor did say I could have one cheat meal a week."

"Dad, I am so done right now. Two things, this is your SECOND cheat meal this week. Yes, mom and I know about the ice cream. And second, I'm telling mom!"

"NO, NO, NO! Alright I'm sorry. It won't happen again."

Brooke bursts out laughing at her father's reaction, which causes him to do the same.

"Don't worry honey, I didn't come this far to screw it all up. I'm going to heed the doctor's strict orders from here on out."

"Thank you, dad, much appreciated."

So, listen, umm… I understand you're going on a date shortly."

"Oh my God, mom promised not to tell. I know how you get."

"No, no, nothing like that. Besides, I hear it's the detective from Florida. I really like him, and I can tell he really likes you."

"Dad, are you serious right now"

"Just do me one favor, honey."

"Sure, what's that?"

"Go out and have a wonderful time. Make sure you give him a chance."

"Thank you, dad, your support means a lot, and I will be certain to give him more than 10 minutes."

Michigan weather remains as unpredictable as the forecasts that precede it. The evening is mild for this time of year, in the low 40's. There hasn't been enough snow to cause any type of accumulation, and almost guarantees a snow-free Christmas holiday. After an extra-long bath, Brooke is now anxious to meet Detective Engler for dinner, though she's having a hard time figuring out why her nerves are trying to get the best of her. She talks to herself in the mirror as she attempts to get ready.

I don't believe I can't pick one stupid top. She rehangs yet another blouse. *It's a simple dinner with a friend. For crying out loud… oh I know… my yellow double-breasted blouse. Problem solved. Alright detective. I'll be there soon!*

Brooke enters the lobby of her favorite sushi restaurant, *Sakana*. She immediately sees Detective Engler. They both smile as they sprightly walk towards each other and hug.

"Wow, look at you, Miss Brooke Hannah. You look wonderful... absolutely wonderful. I was worried about what the Detroit air would do to you, but it's obvious it's had zero affect. And please forgive me for saying this, but you get goo gobs of personal points with me for actually arriving a few minutes early. This never happens."

"You are too funny, detective. It's great to see you in person again. It's been a long time."

"Come on, let's get out of this lobby and have a seat." said the detective. "They already have a booth for us."

The restaurant is quiet this evening with only a few booths occupied. The smell of fresh ginger and citrus cocktails infuse the air. The lighting is subtle and just right for an array of occasions. As usual everything is made to perfection, much to the delight of Detective Engler.

"OK, Brooke, you have done a great job of having me blabber on and on. You're good at this question-and-answer combination."

"I'm sorry detective, it's just that I don't have a whole lot going on. I always like to hear the opposing side. Besides, it's good to hear about my second home."

"Fair enough. I would like to make a request. This is not official business right here and now. This is non-work related and pleasurable for me. Please call me, Brett. No more of this detective stuff."

"Aww. I was really starting to like the detective name too," Brooke said as she mildly blushes. "Well Brett, tell me what you think of my hometown so far."

"I'd say breathtaking and agonizingly beautiful. Detroit is OK too."

Brooke bursts out into laughter and quickly looks down and away from embarrassment.

"No, you didn't just say that!"

"I'm sorry for putting you on the spot like that, Brooke. Well not really sorry for my compliment, but I didn't mean to make your cheeks red."

"Really, Detective Brett Engler? I'm a big girl. I can handle myself."

There is a brief moment of awkward yet flirtatious silence, as they both gaze at each other for a moment.

"It's really not a bad night outside, even for Detroit," said the detective. "Would you like to go for a walk?"

"That sounds like a splendid idea. Let's do it!"

The night air is trying it's best to influence the remainder of moments with the detective and Brooke. It's calm with no reference to a breeze of any kind. The crowd, the cars, and the parking fall into perfect alignment.

"So, tell me Brett, what made you look me up? I'm happy you did, but just curious… I'm a curious kinda girl."

"Hmph… I had been preparing for you to ask me that question, and everything I told myself I would say has escaped me with relative ease. Since you were on the news back home, everyone knew who you were. I remember the first time I saw you covering that smash and grab story. I thought to myself, my God she is beautiful. But it was something else besides that. Your personality was different. You had such an authentic and personal aura. I wondered if I might ever have the chance to meet you.

"When I heard the call that night over the radio when your neighbor passed away, that was my opportunity. I know I told you something slightly different last time, but I had a dual motive. And then, when we were in that crazy ass house together, I felt really close to you, especially when I had you standing directly behind me while we spoke to that psycho's dad.

"We made it through that whole ordeal, and then everything moved so fast. You were traveling and doing talk shows and interviews. The next thing I know; you're moving back to Detroit. This conference that I attended was really meant for the chiefs of police to attend. I begged Chief Jared to let me attend on his behalf. Somehow, I believe he really knew why I wanted to go.

"Brooke, I wanted to see you one more time. I wanted to see your face. I wanted to smell your wonderful perfume. I wanted to just feel close to you again. But also, to let you know that should things change, and you ever decide to come back to Florida, I'm going to do my best detective work and arrest your heart. I give you my word on that."

They both stop, and for a moment of absolute perfection, so does the rest of the world. The detective gently twists her till they are face to face. His right hand gently moves her hair as it flows through his fingers. They both close their eyes and await the conclusion. The detective is gentle and respectful as his lips mesh with hers. It was the kiss that neither of them knew would happen, but both are undeniably pleased that it did. The detective walks her to her car, and they bid each other farewell until next time.

The detective chooses to watch her leave before he gets into his vehicle.

He's cute! Brooke takes another glance through her rearview mirror at the detective that stole a kiss.

Chapter 22

Two Guns

March 14, 2017 2:15PM

K yle, are you sure you wanna do this? It's not too late to step away from this," said Dimitri as he tries to adjust his pillows and sit more upright. "I think we are in over our heads. I really do."

"No worries, cuz. After this job we are done. I promised you before, and I'm not going back on my word. We will be in Amsterdam by same time next week. Look… we will *never* have to come back here. Besides, who better to do contract work with?"

"All money ain't good money is all I'm saying. This guy has too much power, Kyle. Even in Amsterdam he has reach. I don't trust him. Why in the hell would someone like that be involved in this nickel and dime bull? And I don't like this solo shit. Gun one gun two… that's how we've always handled our business. What's the damn hurry anyhow? I still got your back on this."

"Cuz, we're talking about $650,000. This ain't that crazy complicated shit we've done before. These guys have to be discreet. They have to be clean because of who they are… they really have no choice. They came to us because they know we can deliver the best results. And you know damn well as I do that you won't be moving from this bed for at least a few days... *doctor's orders*. We need you to get your strength up enough to hop on that plane."

"Kyle, just answer me this one more time. The target is old as hell. What is he... like 90 years old? He probably already has Alzheimer's or something like that anyway. Why would they be paying us $650,000? Something is not adding up. I couldn't find anything on that old dude. He's a nobody as far as I can tell."

"Cuz, think about our agreement. Who cares who that old ass is? Whoever he is, he must be someone important enough to be snuffed. He must not be too crazy yet. Nobody likes a snitch. I'm sure that's what he is. They already gave us $100,000 as a deposit. You and I verified it's in the account. If they didn't give us a penny more, that's still more than we've gotten for a single job. Look, we are close! This is our last job. I'll be back soon. And you know what? I'm going to bring you one of those fancy donuts you like from Louie's. Get some rest"

"I don't like this shit one bit, but like you said, this is our last job. I can't wait to get back to some real food and genuine women. Everything is fake here. Listen, *you keep it tight*. Clean and tight. Call me as soon as you finish, and you are someplace safe."

3:30pm

As Kyle sits and waits in the field, he sees two black Suburban's pull up in his rearview mirror. *Ok, gentlemen, looks like its show time.* He watches cautiously.

Two men in dark sunglasses and dark suits emerge from each truck. They have the stereotypical agent look about themselves. One of them stays back, as the other approaches Kyle's door.

"Good afternoon Mr. Craiger," said the agent looking man. "Why don't you come on back and join me. He is ready to speak with you. I hope you don't mind, but I'm going to need to commandeer your weapon, and of course I'm sure you wouldn't mind a quick search?"

"No, I understand," said Kyle. "I left my firearm in my car, otherwise I'm clean."

"That you are, Mr. Craiger. Here's your briefcase. It has your credentials, some local maps, and a few files that you'll want to review. Your hotel room has already been taken care of. The key to your room is also inside. You will also find the rest of your money has already been deposited. There is a suit hanging in your closet we especially picked out for you."

"I wasn't expecting the payment before I did the job, but I appreciate your confidence. I won't let you down. Has anything else changed in my instructions?"

"Nothing else has changed, Mr. Craiger. Our level of confidence in your work is exceptionally high. Just retrieve the files and deal with the interference. Make sure it's quick and clean. But then again you're the expert at his right?" The agent cracks a half-smile. "Right this way."

Kyle enters the truck and sits in the backseat next to a familiar face.

"Mr. Craiger it is indeed a pleasure to meet you. I'm a face-to-face type of man, much to the chagrin of my highly capable men."

"Sir, really, the pleasure is all mine. I wanted to…"

"Let's get down to business, Mr. Craiger. First, I appreciate your swiftness in this delicate situation. I have run out of patience with time. Let me ask you a question… do you know why this country is dying?"

"Well not exactly, sir."

"It's dying because we can't see out of these two black eyes we have. Black eyes we've caused because of our own ignorance and arrogance. As we've let things continue to escalate and now plague us, the rest of the world has eaten our dinner off our plates.

"This country is dying because many of us lack the courage to chase that damn word called, *change*. We are not pioneering anymore. We are playing catch up. We are no longer leaders. We are handcuffed followers. And guess what? I have to clean this mess up.

"And this is why you are here. My emergency clean-up plan is in effect. The first order of business is removing one of those black eyes. Your flight leaves in a couple of hours. I want Barnaby Trekker dead. You have 72 hours to make it so. Make sure you read those files you were given thoroughly. It will give you some insight that will boil your blood. I don't tolerate mistakes, Mr. Craiger. There can be no retakes. Do I make myself clear?"

Kyle's body temperature escalates as he clears his throat of confident nerves... "Crystal clear sir!"

Chapter 23

Night at the Museum

March 16, 2017 Holocaust Museum

Barnaby Trekker has a rather important evening lined up for the Holocaust Museum. He has prepared a specially catered dinner and tour of the museum for several out-of-town VIP's, as well as some notable local dignitaries. These private showings typically result in gaining additional funding for the museum. However, hours before his guests arrive, he receives news he must share with Brooke immediately.

"Good morning, Mr. Trekker," said Brooke. "How are you doing?"

"I am doing wonderful Brooke, absolutely wonderful. I just got off the phone with one of my close friends and colleagues, Marko Postair. He is the only other person that has an outside view of the information that I've shared with you. He has been a great life-long friend to both me and Hans. Had he not passed away so quickly the night you met him, I'm certain he would have mentioned Marko's name. I won't go into details over the phone; however, he has given me some information that will help us both out tremendously. I'm committing some details to paper even as we speak. Are you available to drop by the museum anytime tomorrow?"

"Why sure, I am. I wouldn't be available until later in the afternoon. Would that timeline work for you?"

"That is perfect, Brooke. I will be here until around 7pm. I can stay as late as you need. Thank you again for everything. I look forward to our conversation tomorrow."

Mr. Trekker concludes the dinner and tour with his guests. While the majority of them make their way back home or to the airport, there are two guests that still remain. Mr. Trekker invites them to his office for a cocktail.

"Mr. Trekker, I must tell you that I am deeply impressed with what you've been able to accomplish with this museum," said Thomas Copeland. "I visited the DC museum last week. You certainly have the vision. With the right resources and community involvement here, I can certainly see something similar here in Michigan. You've gained an ally my friend. I will be in touch in the upcoming weeks so we can start working out some specifics. And on that note, if you two gentlemen will excuse me, I will bid you adieu."

"Mr. Copeland allow me to walk you out," said Mr. Trekker. "And no rush, Mr. Craiger. Please enjoy your brandy. I shall return."

As Mr. Trekker bids his goodbye to Mr. Copeland, he returns to his office. The museum is calm and quiet, except for Mr. Trekker's brown penny loafers making uneven music with the floor. His limp will not get the best of him today.

"Ah, Mr. Craiger, I see you've taken interest in those pictures. Here, let me walk you through them."

"Certainly, Mr. Trekker, I do appreciate this."

"My pleasure… this one on the left is my dad and his brother… Uncle Silas. The two beautiful ladies in the middle are my mom and one of her best friends, Mrs. Celeste. And that last one on the end…"

"Let me guess that one. That must be you and your wife. You still look the same Mr. Trekker. Your wife's face is so familiar. I've seen it before. I just don't know where."

"How's that, Mr. Craiger? Well, my wife was in the school system. She was an administrator until she retired. But you said you were from Utah, correct? Perhaps just a resemblance. My dear Sarah… it was a lifetime ago when we took that picture together, but I can still feel everything about that day like it just recently happened. May she continue to rest in peace."

"My apologies Mr. Trekker, I didn't…"

"Nonsense. No apologies are necessary. I have many great memories. So how about you, Mr. Craiger. We really didn't get to talk much with the others in attendance earlier. You are much more reserved. You seem to be a fierce thinker. But you're also a young man. Are you married? What got you into this line of work? It is rare to meet someone that more closely resembles my passions these days in the world of antiquity preservation and investments."

"Please call me Kyle, Mr. Trekker," he said, as he has trouble removing his eyes from the picture of Trekker's wife. He feels as though this is certainly no mere resemblance.

"Very well Kyle, and dropping all these boring formalities, I extend the sentiment likewise. Please call me Barnaby." They both smile.

"Well, I'm not married. Perhaps one day. I travel a lot, Barnaby, but I'm looking to settle down. I am young, that much is true. But the miles I've put on this 34 year-old body and the things I've seen have aged me half a lifetime. I'm ready to meet her, whomever she is. One day Barnaby… one day.

"My father left me and my mom when I was still a baby. My mother struggled for many years. I vowed I would make something of myself so my mother would have to struggle no more. Someone gave me an opportunity to invest one day, and the rest is history. My mother lives comfortably and travels the world offering her time to those that are less fortunate. I suppose, in a way, she was just like her mother Alice. My grandmother lost her life during WWII in one of Hitler's concentration camps. Before she died though, she helped so many others."

Mr. Trekker's voice is excitable. "Your grandmother was there? Alice is her first name? What was her last name Kyle?"

"Stern was her last name. Alice Stern was my grandmother."

Mr. Trekker plops down on his desk. Kyle, I know your grandmother. I knew her well!"

"I know you did ,Barnaby. That's one of the reasons I'm here."

Chapter 24

Double Crossed

Mr. Trekker rises from his desk and stares at Kyle with a look of surprise and reluctance. This turn of events is not something he expected. Kyle turns around with a gun and aims it at Mr. Trekker's head.

"What is the meaning of this?" Mr. Trekker slowly backs away from the desk. "How dare you come to me under false pretenses. I knew you weren't an investor of the arts. You lack refinement. You are wasting your time. I have nothing for you. I suggest you Google what you seek or go to one of the local libraries. Now, I'm going to have to ask you to leave. Please don't make me call the police."

Mr. Trekker places his hand on the phone to reinforce his threat.

"I wouldn't use that hand if I were you," said Kyle as he removes a silencer from his jacket pocket and screws it on his firearm.

"You see, in my line of work, I know when I'm being lied to. I also know how to get the answers I need. Now tell me where the flash drive is. I don't want the ones filled with loving memories of your grandkids. I want the one that has the information on Grade X. Now, don't give me any bullshit, just hand it over and do it quickly."

"*Grade X flash drive*? I don't know what you are asking for. You have the wrong person, young man."

"My instructions were actually quite simple. I ask you one question and await your response. If your response is not the right one, I get to plug some bullets into your sorry ass. Guess what? I didn't like your answer," said Kyle as he removes the safety from his firearm.

"WAIT!" said Mr. Trekker as he tries to buy himself some time. "You don't understand. You have the wrong person. I…"

"You are a murderer! Yes, you *do* know my grandmother. You know her because you killed her. She lost her life like so many… millions of others in that goddamn concentration camp. Tell me Mr. Gurbl, how many were you responsible for killing? *That's right*! I know who you really are. You are Enrich Gurbl. A former member of Hitler's SS squad, and one of the commanding officers at Auschwitz. I read every despicable thing about you, Gurbl. Time has run out for you. I've been sent to help you rest in peace you bastard."

"Wait A Minute…Wait a minute."

Mr. Trekker reaches his hand for the guest chair behind him and sits. His body is shaking, and his eyes are swollen trying to hold back the pain and memories of the horrid smells… of all those lives lost. His family, his friends, even those that were enemies.

"No time for sympathy old man. I have things to do and places to go. I earned a nice little sum for this cake job. Time to meet your maker."

"*Please,* before you pull that trigger, just do one thing. I want you to see something. After that, you may carry out your duty. I need to go to my safe. I promise it's nothing suspect. I just need to go behind that statue in the corner."

"This better be good, old man. Make it quick. And I swear if you even breath the wrong way around the damn statue, I'm going to paint it with your brains."

Mr. Trekker gingerly rises, out of breath, and makes his way behind the statue to the left of his desk. He pushes the statue forward, revealing a small square hole beneath it. He removes a small steel safe, which resembles one in which handguns are secured in.

"Like I said before, you make one wrong move, and you are done." Kyle has the gun aimed precisely at Mr. Trekker's head.

Mr. Trekker makes his way back to his desk as Kyle slowly backs away. He enters the combination and removes a small journal. There are other papers of some sort he leaves in the safe. As he opens the journal, it is filled with pictures and letters. His hands are shaking as he shuffles through them. He eventually finds what he's looking for.

"Kyle, please look at these. Study them closely."

Kyles cycles through the pictures and looks up wide-eyed at Mr. Trekker. He looks through the letters and recognizes the names. He takes a few steps closer to the picture of Mr. Trekker and his wife, all the while keeping him in his peripheral.

"What is this? What the hell is this? I don't understand," said Kyle as he throws the pictures back on the desk.

"Kyle, I don't know who sent you here after me, but they are using you. I believe we are both being double-crossed. I'm not a damn Nazi. I'm not a soldier, and I have never held allegiance to Hitler. You recognized my wife in the picture behind me because she took a picture... many pictures with your grandmother. They were best friends. Those pictures I just showed you are of the three of us and your grandfather. He was the first to be killed."

"I don't want to hear this, you're lying."

"I am not lying Kyle, and you will listen. You will hear the truth today."

Kyle slowly lowers his weapon. He's confused, but also still on ready alert.

"Your Grandmother Alice was a great friend to me and my Sarah. It was heartbreaking what they did to her. They were brutal. The real Nazi tyrants raped her for five days straight. It wasn't just one soldier, sometimes it was up to four different soldiers going one after the other. If that wasn't enough, they also beat her before, during, and after they gang-raped her. She was in such bad shape. They didn't bother with her on that sixth day. We all tried to help her, but her mind was so damaged emotionally that she shunned us.

"The day after, one of the careless soldiers decided he wanted to enjoy a solo mission with Alice. Something was different about her on that day. No more than ten minutes later, we all heard the soldier scream in agony, followed by a single gunshot. That gunshot killed your grandmother. We later found out that she removed something from the soldier that he used to hold dearly. I won't go into the details, as I'm sure you understand. He later died from excessive bleeding.

"Kyle, I have so many stories similar to the one I just told you. I have spent my life trying to reunite with those that survived that hell. I am no soldier or Nazi no more than you are. Thank goodness Hitler and his mad scheme weren't successful. Otherwise, your mother and so many others would never have had the opportunity to exist. Tell me... how many of Hitler's men wore this?"

Mr. Trekker reveals the infamous Auschwitz tattoo on his left forearm, which consists of six numbers.

"This is my arm jewelry, my regalia, my only tattoo. Some were lucky enough to wear them only in their clothing. I was not one of the lucky ones. I look at the tattoo daily. And you know what? Each day brings back those memories with vivid clarity. These tattoos were synonymous with the prisoner's camp number. Sometimes they would add a special symbol.   For instance, some Jews had a triangle. I never knew what they symbolized, and it really didn't make a difference... Why? Because in a way we weren't any different than cattle being led to slaughter. Would you like to hear some explicit details, Kyle?"

Kyle completely relaxes his gun. He removes the silencer and holsters both. He picks up the pictures on the desk and cycles through them once again. He is now completely unsettled. Mr. Trekker continues to shake, though now more pronounced.

"No, I don't need any more details. Like I said before, I know when I'm being lied to, or at least I thought I did. You are telling the truth and that's for sure. But that slick bastard… none of this makes sense."

"Kyle, please pass me my jacket hanging up on the coat rack."

Kyle reaches for the burgundy corduroy blazer. Mr. Trekker is shaking slightly more as he receives his blazer and starts reaching into the inside breast pocket.

"Who sent you hear Kyle? Why… why me?"

"Who, is no longer important, Barnaby. They planted me with false evidence. Whatever this Grade X mumbo jumbo is, they are ready to have you dead over it."

"But I have nothing they would need. Yeah, I'm a person that knows a few details that others don't, but the things they need the most are not with me. I search for the same answers I'm afraid."

"What is Grade X Barnaby? What would happen if this stuff landed in the wrong hands?"

Mr. Trekker continues to fumble through his pockets, his face starting to turn pale.

"The fact that someone is looking for this here and now after so many years is troubling. Grade X is the end of the world in the wrong hands. You are in way over your head. The people your work for… they will kill you. You must remain as ignorant about this subject matter as you already are. But that might be too late anyway. Did something fall on the floor over there?" Mr. Trekker looks worried.

Kyle looks back along the floor tracing it back to the coat rack. Nothing fell Barnaby... what's wrong? You're not looking good."

"Old age and forgetfulness, Kyle. I need my... I believe I left my medicine on my kitchen counter."

Mr. Trekker starts taking more deliberate and deep breaths. His hands are now shaking uncontrollably.

"What is it? What's happening?" as Kyle walks beside Mr. Trekker.

"My heart... *it's my heart*. Listen to me, there is little time. I need to ask you a favor."

Mr. Trekker now sounds like he just ran up a flight over stairs. His brow is moist from sweat. His chest rises and falls like turbulent waves crashing about in the ocean.

"Please Kyle... a favor for an old family friend."

"OK, OK, what is it? What can I do?"

"In my safe," he pants ever more heavily. "In my safe is a letter for Brooke... Brooke Hannah. Please make sure she gets it. And you Ky ---- Kyle. Take those pictures. They were taking during some truly happy times for all of us. Whatever you are involved in, you must walk away from it. Your mission is accomplished my dear boy. Go ---- live! Don't forget the..."

Mr. Trekker's head collapses backward in his chair, as it gently caresses the wall and portrait of him and his wife.

"Shit! Shit! What the hell is this? What am I involved in? Who the hell is, Brooke Hannah? I gotta get out of here.

Trekker was never the one that needed a bullet in the head you bastard. Mr. Fucking man. You are a slick bastard. But I got my money. I hope I live to spend it. Hang in there, cuz. We are almost home free."

Chapter 25

Unfinished Business

Kyle quickly leaves the museum. He is confused, angry and paranoid. There was no way Trekker was lying. But he couldn't understand why they would intentionally deceive him by giving him erroneous information. *They coulda kept all that extra spy bullshit,* he thought. Being a person with power brings with it many luxuries. In this case, the ability to provide or manipulate information.

He walks quickly to his parked car, but something is unsettling. His paranoia has gotten the best of him. He stands there staring at his car like it had morphed into something completely unrecognizable. He looks around quickly, panning the area, but he knows if anyone is watching him it's from a safe distance. He backs away from the black Nissan Altima rental and makes his way back to the entrance of the museum. You don't become the best in your field by miscalculating the odds and risks.

Kyle opens his briefcase and sits it on the ground, removing something from it that resembles a remote. When you do hit and reconnaissance missions, you gain friends in high and unfamiliar places. The device is his hands was given to him by one of his inside people at NATO. It is called a *Trail Gun*, which is a nonlethal gun that emits a beam of microwave energy that causes voltage spikes in electronic devices, essentially frying the circuits within. He aims the trail gun at the Altima and engages it. Nothing happens!

Well, what in the hell do you know! I guess I should thank you assholes for allowing me to drive my car in peace. Oh wait... shit, all the circuits are fried. I can't drive this damn thing anymore. Alright whatever! I'll find a damn cab or UBER driver.

He removes the shiny silver briefcase from the trunk, with the bogus information on Trekker. He walks down Orchard Lk Rd. as he immediately sees a cab parked just across the street. He waves his hands. The taxi driver rolls down his window.

"Hey, pal I need ride pronto."

"I'm not for hire right now, I..."

Kyle reaches into his pocket. "How about $100 bucks to drive me to the Sheraton in Novi?"

"Hop in my good man. I will get you there quickly," said the taxi driver with an immediate smile and interest.

As Kyle arrives at the hotel, the same paranoia is still ever present. He quickly makes his way inside and to his room. Everything is in order with nothing out of place or suspicious. He calls the number given to him by the agent to report his job completion.

"Mr. Craiger, it's nice to hear from you," said the man on the other end. "We were beginning to get a little anxious. Are your activities completed as instructed?"

"Yes. Everything is calm and quiet. Mr. Trekker is resting comfortably."

"Very good, Mr. Craiger. And what about the file?"

"It's not a file. It's some old journal. I will place it in the drop-off as instructed. We are square now, right?"

"As long as that journal is what we seek, we are fair and square. I need you to take a few pictures of this journal and send it to me. I will call you back once we've reviewed them."

Kyle takes several pictures of the Goebells' journal and sends them to the agent. Less than five minutes later, the agent calls him back...

"Mr. Craiger, what did Trekker tell you about Project Grade X?"

"He said everything he knew was in this journal."

"This was not what we were quite looking for; however, what you've given us is something we didn't know existed. I take it a bullet to the head was the end of your conversation with Trekker?"

"Actually, it was a lot cleaner than that. He died from a heart attack moments after I put the gun to his head. There won't be any questions or investigations with this one."

There is a moment of silence on the other end of the line. Kyle can hear his own heart pacing frantically.

"Very well, Mr. Craiger. Consider your task complete. Drop off that valuable relic at the agreed upon spot, and enjoy your earnings. We'll be in touch."

"There's no need, I'm..." The line goes dead before Kyle could finish his sentence. He unclips another cell phone from his waist and dials his cousin Dimitri.

"Kyle, is it you?"

"It's me cuz, I'm done. Are you OK? No problems?"

"Dude what the fuck. Yes, I'm fine... what took you so long? You said this was a cake job."

"Calm down, calm down. I needed an extra day to make the right preparations. You know how I hate that role-playing crap anyway."

"So, you are safe? The job... was it clean? Was it up to standard?"

"Clean like smooth ass, cuz. The money is already deposited into our account. We are good to go. How's those legs doing? I'm flying back tomorrow evening, then we need to get everything together, and guess what? We're off to Amsterdam after that. We are done cuz. We are finally done!"

"Kyle... I have waited a long time to celebrate this. These shit jobs were never for us. We did what we had to do I guess, but there's been too much blood man. Too many times where we did it and didn't really understand why we did it. But that's over now, right?"

"Yes, it's over now. We will relax and spend plenty of time fishing. Start getting yourself together. We will be on our way soon."

9:00am the next morning

Kyle spends the morning reading about Brooke Hannah. He feels unconnected somehow, as he was totally oblivious to everything that has happened surrounding her name in the past couple of years. He honor's one of Mr.

Trekker's dying wishes. Attached to the envelop he is to deliver to Brooke is one of her business cards. He calls her personal cell phone number.

"Hello, Brooke Hannah speaking."

"Hello, Miss Brooke Hannah. Listen, you don't know me, and I really don't have time to give you my life story. My name is Kyle, and Mr. Trekker asked me to give you something. It's an envelope with your name on it."

"Umm Kyle, why can't Mr. Trekker give it to me himself?" Brooke braces herself for the response.

"Mr. Trekker died of a heart attack late yesterday evening. Where can I meet you to give you this envelope?"

"Oh no…" Brooke is distraught.

This whole story, this whole scenario is taking on a familiar theme that she doesn't like. She doesn't know who Kyle is and can't trust meeting him. Besides she doesn't want to place Charlie in any potential harm.

Charlie motions to Brooke. "Are you OK?"

"Yes, I'm fine," said Brooke as she mutes her handset. "I tell you what Kyle. If you can drop it off at the news station with the security guard, I will phone ahead to let him know to look out for you. Listen, are you sure about Mr. Trekker?"

"Suit yourself. Where is your office located? And yes, I am quite sure. He seemed like a nice guy."

"550 W. Lafayette Blvd in Detroit. How do you know Mr. Trekker?" There is silence on the other end. "Hello!" The call had already been disconnected.

"What the heck was that all about?"

"I don't know Charlie... I don't know!"

1:30pm

Kyle does some shopping for him and his cousin at the local mall. For the first time in many years, he feels a sense of completion. There is a brief period of doubtfulness and uncertainty that overcomes him, thinking about what he and his cousin will do next. But it quickly dissipates with the feeling of knowing whatever choices they make from here on out, they won't involve any of the illegal and illicit activities that had become a major part of their lives. His phone rings as he makes his way back to his car.

"Yo cuz, hold on minute. Let me put these bags in the trunk." There is a brief pause. "What's up man? I just finished picking us up a few things for the trip back. You ready? How you feelin boss?"

There is a bout of silence before Dimitri speaks. "What kind of shopping did you do?"

"I picked up some shirts and pants, oh and I picked up a couple of hats. Just some stuff to hold us over until we get home. I was thinking..."

"Listen Kyle, I need to tell you something. When you called me last night, I had gotten a call earlier that morning. Dr. Lukar wanted me to come in, but I told him no. You know how you have that sick feeling in your stomach. He was still pissed at me for leaving the hospital in the first place, but you know how I feel about those places. The swelling has gone down in my legs, and the infection is going away. But you know me... there's gotta be some extra drama involved."

"Drama... extra drama? What the hell are you talking about, cuz?"

"The doctor told me the cancer is back. It's back like a sonofabitch Kyle. Listen man, there's nothing they can do."

"Wait a minute! What do you mean there's nothing they can do? What are you saying?"

"I might have anywhere from three to six months with the way it's spreading. You wanna hear something? I'm not scared at all. Not even nervous about it. I'm pissed. I'm pissed because we made it through all this bullshit all these years. Bullets, falls, pain, and even tears. We went through all of that, and now I get took down from some shit I can't battle. No matter what I do, I can't win this fight. This is so fucked up right now. Listen Kyle, my cousin... my best damn friend, in this hellhole. I need you to do me a favor."

Kyle is sitting in the parking lot of the mall with both hands on the steering wheel staring out the windshield. The car keys resting lonely on the passenger seat.

"Anything, cuz. You know you don't have to ask twice. What do you need?"

"I need you to go to our new home in Amsterdam. Stay far away from this life we have lived these last 15 years. Settle down. You are an old man now. You need a wife."

"Dimitri... cuz, wait a minute."

"No Kyle, listen to me bro. Everything is clear right now. Buy those fishing poles you and me talked about. Maybe one day you can have a son and teach him how to do it. I'm not making this trip. I'm too tired. I refuse to go out like this. You take care of yourself cousin. I love you man. Please don't come back to this apartment. I don't want you to see... Goodbye!"

"*Cuz wait*! CUZ ..." The line goes silent as Kyle dials Dimitri's phone repeatedly. It keeps going straight to voicemail. Fuck, Fuck, Fuck!" Kyle pounds his fist into the steering wheel. He knows that was the last time for him and Dimitri. They grew up poor and against the odds, and rose to become some of the best for-hire assassins in the game. They never liked that term, instead referring themselves to *Solutions Experts*. The pain is long and blistering, but Kyle forces himself to pick up the keys and drive off to the airport. His life from this day forward would celebrate what he and his cousin Dimitri desired most... peace.

Chapter 26

Patience is a Virtue

"Pardon me sir, may I interrupt?"

"You may. Do you come with news about Trekker?"

"Yes sir, I do. Trekker is dead."

"Well, that is good news. I don't normally get excited over dead people, but this one brings a smile to my face. No more snooping around for that old pain in the ass. Ok, give me the great news."

"Well, sir, that's where there's a slight problem."

"Hear me well on this; this will be the only time I repeat it. On this level, there are no slight problems."

"Y-yes sir, understood. Mr. Craiger retrieved a journal from Trekker. There was no flash drive, no computer data, or for that matter, anything on Grade X."

"Hmph! So, what's the journal all about?"

"It is the long rumored lost journal of the Reich Minister of Propaganda for the Nazi Party, Joseph Goebbels. There is no reference to Grade X, only his disillusionment with Adolf Hitler."

"Come again? What do you mean disillusionment? If I can remember my history lessons, I was taught that Goebbels was one of his most trusted confidants, next to Albert Speer."

"I seem to remember the same thing sir. Maybe this changes up history somewhat."

The man sitting behind the desk laughs hysterically.

"So, let me get this straight. I paid Kyle Craiger $650,000 for killing an old man and getting me a journal that says Hitler and Goebbels might not have been best buds after all?"

"Sir, I'm sorry, I…"

"You know what? It doesn't matter at this point. It just proves that Trekker was fishing. He didn't have anything of relevance. But, he's still much better out of the picture than causing any chaos. You know what else? Something tells me he may have another voice out there. I'm sure we will find out whom shortly. And rest assured, we will *kill them* too!"

Chapter 27

The Last Letter

This entire day for Brooke has been surreal and sad. Not long after her conversation with Kyle, Mr. Trekker's death is breaking news on all the local channels. Since she was covering another important story clear across town, one of her colleagues takes the story. There were no signs of foul play. Initial reports suggested that he died the way Kyle said he did.

She thinks back to when she first was introduced to Mr. Trekker by her grandfather. His smile and mannerisms stayed exactly the same. His voice was always soft and unexcitable. It seemed that each word formed in his mouth was full of wisdom.

She had never heard Mr. Trekker mention anyone by the name of Kyle. She doesn't want to believe he died from a heart attack. None of this sits right. Perhaps the letter would give her some clues. She makes her way back to the news station at the completion of her last story, albeit with reluctance. The letter addressed to her lies sitting on her desk. It simply has her first name written across the front of it. Her hands tremble gently as she starts to read it.

"Here are some details on paper for what we discussed. If I don't write things down these days, I tend to forget them. This is much too important to forget. Thank goodness to Marko for really coming through for us. I know he will be happy to meet you. I will make arrangements for this to happen. Heinz Gruber goes by the name of Johnny Marshall. His address is 300 N. Cattail Rd. Lincoln, NE. He stays by himself and from what Marko says, looks remarkably youthful for his age. No doubt some bonus side effects of Grade X."

Trekker

She carefully refolds the letter and places it in her purse. *Mr. Trekker, I hope you didn't die because of this letter. Where does all this lead?*

March 19, 2016 the next morning

Brooke decides to get an early morning Saturday workout. After that and a Bikram Yoga class, she feels refreshed and recharged. On the drive back home, she receives a call she's been waiting for.

"Oh my God I swear I was just thinking of you earlier today," said Brooke. "What's going on with you, chickie?"

"Hey girly, same ole, same ole," said Agent Lana Quiver. "How are you doing? Listen, I'm so sorry it's taken me so long to get back to you."

"Please girl, no worries. I can only imagine how busy you've been. The bad guys keep us employed, don't they?"

"Yes, they do. There is no time for boredom that's for sure. Summer is coming around, and we haven't made any hang out plans yet."

"I know, right!? Well, I think it's high time we did something about that."

"I'm going to be taking a long weekend in April. Maybe I can fly over to Detroit and hang out with you for a couple of days. We can make plans then. And maybe if we plan it right, Carla might be able to join us."

"That would be awesome. Let me know the exact dates, and I will clear my schedule."

"I will for sure. I will call you back sometime next week. So, listen the reason for my call. I have some information for you on Reina."

"Really? That's great! What did you find out?"

"First off, I'm going to say this as your friend and enforcement agent. I'm not sure what you are working on, but please be careful with this information you are receiving. Sometimes you can piss people off in the wrong places. This thing is weird to me, but I'm not asking any questions. If you need me, don't hesitate to call. Is there something we should discuss now?"

"No chickie… not yet at least. I promise I won't go running off on a tangent. I learned my lesson from last time."

"OK, I'm going to hold you to that. So, there was only one person with the name of Reina that traveled to Germany during that time. Her name was Reina Santini. And remember when we spoke last, I told you she had a twin brother? Well, his name was Rainier. They both traveled to Germany via a flight from France on December 17, 1943. They both returned to the US on July 12, 1945. I have no other records on either of them. It's like they vanished after they returned home. I do have one more thing, which might be just coincidental, but Reina had a striking resemblance to Hitler's short-lived wife, Eva Braun. They could pass for the same woman. It's really odd. Is that what your story is about? The resemblance?"

"Wow, no not at all, but that is wonderful information. This helps me out a great deal."

"If you say so. I'm not sure how, but just be careful with this information. Listen I gotta run, but I will call you late next week so we can cement those plans for April."

The call ends as Brooke arrives at her apartment.

This story is getting crazier by the minute. She goes inside and crash lands on her yellow tufted leather sofa. She reaches into her purse and reads the letter from Mr. Trekker once again. *Looks like Reina made it back home Mr. Trekker. I'll do my best to figure this thing out so it can be laid to bed. I really should have been a private investigator. Looks like I need to make a trip to Nebraska. This should be interesting.*

Chapter 28

Down on the Farm

April 1, 2017

One of the additional things that Brooke has come to appreciate about being back home is the deal that she was able to work out during her negotiation with WDIV, where she was able to keep all of her personal time and actually accrued a few more days. She uses a few of them to take an extended weekend and flies to Nebraska. She was unsuccessful in finding any phone contact information on Gruber's new name. In these situations, sometimes a drop-in visit is needed.

Even with everything that she's been through in Florida, she decides to make this trip alone, as she's still not sure what all this information means. She has a sense of safety in visiting this aging man. She can't quite put her finger on why.

She casually drives her rental vehicle down the unusually quite road. There are acres of beige colored fields with the most amazing smell of fresh air. Although city life and its landscape provide her with the fulfillment she desires, she could see herself living in a place like this one day. Kinda isolated from the rest of the world and in obvious peace. A peace that she's about to break. This would be a trip that Brooke would never forget.

She pulls up and knocks on the front door. A warming voice responds, "Who is it?"

"Hello there, my name is Brooke. I'm looking for Mr. Johnny Marshall."

"Well, look no further you've found him," he said as he opens the door.

Just as was stated in Mr. Trekker's letter, he looks amazing for someone in their late eighties. He could surely pass for someone in his fifties, and even that is being conservative. His frame is well built and upright, maybe 6'2" and around 170lbs. His full head of slicked back hair has salt and pepper streaks racing throughout it. But his eyes are different. You can tell that he's seen a lot.

"It's a pleasure to meet you, Mr. Marshall. This place is amazing. Is it always this quiet?"

"Why, yes, it is. I have been here for nearly 70 years. I have had my fair share of traveling, but this place is where I enjoy it the most. The older I get the fonder I grow of it. So where do you stay? Are you not far from around here?"

"Well, I'm actually…"

"Oh, please forgive me, Brooke, right?

"Yes sir, that's correct."

"Where are my manners? Please come in and make yourself at home. Can I interest you in some tea? I have hot or cold. I've never been much of a coffee drinker."

"Why sure, Mr. Marshall, I would love some hot tea only if you intend on joining me."

"Well, you have a deal young lady. Have a seat or feel free to take a look around while I get us squared away."

Brooke looks around the rustic styled home. There are many pictures that line the walls. They look to be hand painted and are all of birds.

"Did you paint these pictures on the wall, Mr. Marshall? They are beautiful."

"Why yes, I did, and thank you kindly. My wife enjoyed the wonderful birds of Nebraska. Her favorite was the Sandhill Crane. That's those three on the far wall. She's been gone for almost 20 years now."

"I'm sorry Mr. Marshall."

"No need to be sorry. We are all moving down the same road. We will each have a turn. Some sooner than others I suppose. All that time together and we never had any kids. We traveled and saw so many beautiful things. Before you knew it, we were both past the age where we felt comfortable having them. But it was difficult for her to have them anyway. Things worked out the way they were supposed to. So where are you from again?"

He returns with an antique silver tray lined with a ceramic tea kettle, two cups, cream, and sugar.

"If you need any more fixins just let me know."

"No, this is perfect. Thank you so much for preparing it."

They both prepare their tea, and Brooke takes a sip before returning to his question.

"I don't stay around here at all. I'm from Detroit, MI."

"*Detroit, MI,*" he said with a confused look on his face. "If you're from Detroit, what on earth are you doing here? Are you at the wrong house young lady?"

"No, I'm at the right house. I want to ask you some questions. Some questions about your life a long time ago."

"Wait a minute, who are you, young lady?"

"My apologies, Mr. Marshall. Where are my manners? My full name is Brooke Hannah. I am a news reporter with WDIV in Detroit."

"A news reporter? Well, this is a first. I have never met a reporter. Why on earth are you here? What could possibly be interesting enough about me that would warrant a visit all the way from Detroit? You said my life from a long time ago? Who sent you? I'm awfully confused about this."

"Were you in the war, Mr. Marshall? Were you in WWII?"

"The war!? No, I never served in the military. I'm afraid you came to the wrong location young lady. Feel free to enjoy a cup of tea or two, but I'm afraid I'm not going to able to offer you too much else."

Brooke knew at some point she was going to have to ask the tough questions. She figures now is as good a time as any.

"You were born in Germany, correct?"

"No, I was born here. It is true that my parents were German, but I was born here. I still have a very small accent, but that's as German as I get."

"With the utmost respect sir, I know you weren't born here in the United States. When did you come over? Was it before or after Adolph Hitler took his life?"

"I beg your pardon! Well, you've just talked yourself out of another cup of tea. And if you keep it up, I'm going to have to ask ..."

"Your name is Heinz Gruber. You were Hitler's only test subject. You have Grade X chemicals in your body. You *were* the original SS. Keeping in line with respect, does that now ring a bell?"

His face is raw, his eyes are stunned, and his mouth is agape. Thousands upon thousands of images rush through his mind. He didn't notice that he'd dropped his cup of tea to the hardwood floor. Heinz Gruber was buried nearly 70 years ago. And now he's back.

"Who are you? You are more than a reporter. How do you know that name? Who sent you here?"

"My apologies, sir. I hope I didn't upset you. Here, allow me to clean this up. May I get a paper towel from the kitchen?"

He sits there motionless, unable to speak or move. Brooke rises and goes to the kitchen to retrieve paper towel and finds something suitable to scoop up the shattered pieces from the teacup strewn all over the floor.

"I am a reporter Mr.... what would you prefer for me to call you now? Mr. Gruber or Mr. Marshall?"

He pauses... "Please tell me who sent you, Miss Hannah."

"I was sent here to find you by someone whom you don't know. Someone that just recently passed away. His name was Barnaby Trekker. He was a holocaust survivor. I believe you might know his closest friend, however. His name was Hans Albrecht. He worked closely with Albert Speer at the height of the war. Does that name sound familiar?"

"So, you still assume I'm this Heinz Gruber?"

"I know you are Heinz Gruber. Please allow me to assure you that I am not here on behalf of any law enforcement agencies, or special interest groups. I represent only myself. The reason I'm here is to ask for your help. Both men that I previously mentioned are both deceased now. They died from natural causes; however, they both died wanting me to intercede in something I do not understand. They both believed that something is going to happen with Grade X, and that we are destined for WWIII if we don't avert it. I'm not sure why they chose me to assist with this. I'm hoping you can help me fill in the blanks."

"I do suppose you've proved your legitimacy in the few words you've spoken. I prefer to be called Mr. Marshall. Heinz Gruber died a lifetime ago. But yes, Miss Hannah, he still lives inside of me. That damned chemical and all those experiments are a reminder daily of what I am and who I've become. I want to give you some advice. You are on the cusp of something much larger than you and me. This presents you the perfect opportunity to make your departure and take with you a mystery. If you continue, you will open a dangerous gate that can never be closed."

"Mr. Marshall, the only thing I know right now is that there are many pieces of this puzzle. I haven't identified all the pieces, and I have no idea what the completed picture will look like. If my involvement can avert a certain disaster, I will do whatever I can. We... all of us are worth that sacrifice."

"You speak like a soldier, Miss Hannah. Well spoken words. I will help you open the gate. You're going to be here for a while. I hope you didn't make any dinner plans."

"Not at all, Mr. Marshall. Dinner here sounds wonderful. I can't think of a better meal companion."

"Well, thank you for flattering an old man, Miss Hannah. War is certainly imminent. There is one major reason it will happen. Before we get into that, I think for context you need to understand how I became involved in all of this."

Chapter 29

Army of One

Mr. Marshall and Brooke retreat to the family room. He leaves and returns with a mildly worn accordion file and places it on the table in front of them. He lights several candles and returns to his olive leather chaise.

"My wife burned candles every single day. She thoroughly enjoyed the fragrances and felt they gave her a since of calm and serenity. I have been doing the same every day since she passed away. I love the calmness, but more than anything else, I can feel her right here next to me."

"I have to agree with you and your wife. I also light candles daily. They are a major part of my calming sanctuary."

Mr. Marshall nods and smiles. He looks around the room for a moment, as if waiting for something to happen.

"Adolf Hitler was an absolute genius. The knowledge that he amassed, the teams of other geniuses that were put together, and the many secrets many have never known make him one of the greats in human history. But he will never be known for his genius. He will forever live on in the minds of many as a tyrant and diabolical maniac. And please make no mistake about it, there were things he did that many of us did not support. The mass extermination was one of them. Tell me, have you ever heard of the Hitler Youth, Miss Hannah?"

"Yes, I have. They were young soldiers that fought in the war. I believe some of them were quite young... some as young as 17 years old."

"There were some as young as 14 actually. At one point, the Hitler Youth totaled more than 8 million members. All those kids being trained to be killers. The youth were all delusional. We thought we could single-handedly help Germany win the war. The truth of the matter was we were just kids with no real front line battle experience. No amount of training or scenarios would be able to save us. We were going to be slaughtered, and even as it became more and more of a reality, so many of us remained steadfast to the Fuhrer's command. I was one of those kids, but I was one with special privileges. My father was Otto Gruber, one of Hitler's top scientists. It was my father that was instrumental in the development of Grade X. I should probably tell you what Grade X is and isn't first."

Mr. Marshall pulls a photo from the accordion folder and hands it to Brooke.

"That's a picture of me, my father, and the face the whole world knows, Mr. Adolf Hitler. That picture was taken just after the announcement of the Grade X testing. Grade X originated as a byproduct of treating Hitler's disease. I'm sure you've heard that German scientists were much more advanced than others in their field, especially during his reign. I would like to correct that by stating that was a gross understatement of how vastly superior they were.

"You see, it wasn't until after WWII any research was published on manic-depressive illness. Today we call it bi-polar disorder. In 1938, German scientist Piper Guntalf was investigating the effects of various compounds on patients who exhibited similar behavior of manic-depressive psychosis. In 1939, he discovered lithium carbonate could be used as a successful treatment of manic-depressive psychosis. But with all that research, Fuhrer Hitler was not impressed. He would not allow Piper to administer the lithium treatments. Instead, he came up with a well thought out idea, as he was in a bit of a quandary. The Hitler Youth soldiers were quite efficient, yet they were unable to match the stamina and prowess of many of the older adult soldiers. Hitler asked Piper and my father for assistance. Their job was to create a serum that could be administered to the youth that would make them the ultimate killing machines, and that's where I came in."

"So, wait a minute," Brooke sits astutely. "Hitler was bi-polar? Did he ever receive any treatment for his condition?"

"None whatsoever. He was much too arrogant to view it as an illness. He viewed it as genius. He was a huge Beethoven fan, not many knew this. He considered him a genius and in doing so, carried out his commands with what he called *Classical Precision*, which was in tribute to the late German composer.

"So, all those years and his mental health though recognized, went completely untreated," said Brooke. "It makes me wonder how certain events would have transpired if he were treated. Would he develop even more clarity and cause even more death and destruction or would he have never advanced. But there was still hatred in his heart Mr. Marshall. I'm not sure any medicine would be able to penetrate deep enough to cure that.

"That is one of those fascinating unknowns I suppose, Miss Hannah. Today, there are many cases where someone is diagnosed with certain mental issues early on, and they can still function at a very high level with the proper medication and support. But if their condition were never treated and left unchecked, I suppose our society would be completely different."

Mr. Marshall takes out another picture and hands it to Brooke.

"These were my friends, my young brother in arms. They were to be the other test subjects. But Hitler didn't want to risk testing any unknown agents on large sums of his youth army. He decided to go the research route and do a number of tests on one subject. If everything proved successful, he would roll it out to all his soldiers, even the adults.

"Piper and my father started their experiments on lab mice. They created a new compound they called rexonium. This chemical displayed some phenomenal properties by itself. It was an exceptionally stable formula, that when combined with other agents, produced remarkable results. It was through their scientific brilliance they developed the first synthetic form of testosterone. When they paired it with rexonium, the lab mice all recorded an amazing increase in speed, strength, and heightened senses.

"After only six months of research with the lab mice, Hitler was immensely impressed, but also extremely impatient. Against Piper and my father's best wishes and judgement, he ordered them to administer the cocktail, which was codenamed Grade X, to me immediately."

"So, Grade X is not about a bomb, but some type of exclusive steroid?" asked Brooke looking perplexed.

"Oh no, my dear girl. It's not just about steroids. Remember, rexonium proved to be a stable agent that can be used in the form of a binder with many different agents. It enhances whatever it's paired with. Grade X had many things associated with it. It became an umbrella, with a subset of projects beneath it. I was under the *Human Enhancement* category of Grade X."

"Thank you for the clarification, Mr. Marshall, I believe I understand now. My apologies for the interruption."

"Not at all. You're going to learn some things today that will challenge many of the things you once believed in. So here I am 14 years old and being shot up with something that had never been tested on a human. I was given 15cc of Grade X daily via injectables. They tested my speed, endurance, strength, and mental acuity. By the 30-day mark, I had a marked increase in strength. I was able to overhead press a barbell loaded with 200lbs. By day 90, I was able to easily pick up well over 450 lbs. I crushed every single metric and measurement in each category. I could outlift, outrun, and outsmart all of Hitler's soldiers, even the adults.

All of this and zero side effects. My body was alive. I felt invincible. I could do anything I wanted, and with minimal effort.

"The research was proving to be triumphant. But it came to a halt quickly. The war was raging on, and it was becoming clear we were losing. There was no time to create enough of the magical cocktail and administer it to even a small number of soldiers. The research was not abandoned; it was placed on hold. I'll never forget my last conversation with Hitler, before I made it to America. It was April 30, 1945 in Sweden."

Brooke interjects quickly. "*What a minute,* Mr. Marshall. Surely you don't mean April 30th. That's the day he died… and at the Chancellery if memory serves."

"I am not mistaken about the date nor location. This is where it gets interesting."

Chapter 30

Trading Places

As the evening draws near, Mr. Marshall and Brooke enjoy a nice dinner of homemade Shepard's Pie. As they return to the family room after dinner, he takes out two more pictures and lays them out in front of Brooke.

"Everyone knows the face of that man," he said pointing to the photo of Adolf Hitler which remained in pristine condition. "The person in the other photo you are unaware of, but nonetheless, he was one of the most influential people of our time. His name was Rainier Santini."

Brooke looks up from the picture quickly. "Hey wait a minute. I know that name… I know that name. He had a twin sister named Reina, correct?"

Mr. Marshall is completely stunned. "Why yes… yes he did. How do you know this?"

"I've been working with some friends in high places trying to put this odd story together. I know they traveled to Germany together and returned, but that's where my trail ends. Something tells me you're going to say why."

"I am indeed. Sweden was one of the few countries that were able to maintain complete neutrality throughout the war. They aided both the Germans and the allies during

WWII. This was a perfect place to meet. I was taken to one of their military bases accompanied by my father. I entered a room inside one of the buildings. Once inside, Fuhrer Hitler sat in a high back chair smoking a cigar, his back turned toward me and my father. My father's colleague Piper Guntalf was already present and gave my father some documents to look over.

"The Fuhrer's voice was angry at first. He asked me if I understood all the chaos and all of the deaths that surrounded me. I remember my voice shaking when I told him I did not. He told me it was because of bigots. He said these bigots wanted to have it all. They wanted to undermine all the hard work and sacrifice he did for his mother Germany. He told me that Germany failed today, but that our cause would live on. He said one day the world would again bend at their knees, and when it happens, there would be no mercy.

"I remember my father looking through all of the documents that Piper had given him. He suddenly smiled. The Fuhrer continued. His voice was much calmer now. He thanked me for being so brave and for helping to advance medical technology that was many years ahead of anything anyone else was doing in the world. Hearing that gave me a sense of accomplishment. I felt like I was the central part of something the world had never seen.

"The Fuhrer took a few more puffs of his cigar and asked my father if he liked what he saw on paper. My father was ecstatic. He had never seen this test data before. You see, Hitler's scientists were broken up into several divisions.

Each division was working on groundbreaking research. Some of the research was completely independent. But there were some key projects where the data spilled over into each other.

One of these projects was called *Trading Places*. Piper worked in three different scientific divisions. One of those was the advancement of reconstructive surgery. The father of modern plastic surgery is generally considered to have been Sir Harold Gillies. Let me go on record to say that is completely wrong. Sir Harold Gillies traveled from New Zealand to Germany in 1915 to work directly with Piper, who had already done many successful skin graft and nose reconstruction jobs from those involved in WWI related injuries. But enough of that!

"I am sure I have used the word genius many times since we've started this conversation. But I still feel as though I am giving the term a disservice. What Fuhrer Hitler concocted will never be replicated. In every part of the world, including the United States, Hitler has sympathizers. He had gained a following... mind you a rather impressive and influential following. These followers created Nazi cells across the world. These same cells still exist today, and I'm not talking about Neo Nazi groups and all that other extremist stuff. I'm talking about the wealthy, politicians, doctors, lawyers, you name it. Perhaps even your next-door neighbor back in Detroit. If he were alive today, I am sure he would be astonished on how this network has grown.

"So, wait a minute. I am aware of some of the extremist groups, and even the pockets of those that believed in everything Hitler did, including the mass extinction in the concentration camps. But what makes you believe it is much bigger than this?"

"I am an old man, but I still keep my ear to the ground from time to time. This whole thing is a large tentacled monster that is ready to squeeze the life out of everyone that opposes. This network of people folds neatly into this story. There was a call that went throughout this same network from the Fuhrer himself back in early 1943. He was looking for two individuals who would be essential to his research. His requirements were that he had one male and one female. They needed to be between the ages of 18 and 20. And finally, that they were fluent in English and German. He found the perfect volunteers in the fall of 1944. They were twin siblings Reina and Rainier Santini. They were both independent, having lost their parents in a fire when they were 17. They were also both incredibly intelligent. Despite all the other WWII heroes, it was Hitler that garnered their full attention. They arrived in Germany in late December of that year.

"I remember the first time I met the girl. I wondered why they were bringing Eva by the lab, but then they introduced her as Reina. Her resemblance was remarkable. They could have easily been identical twins. Reina's hair was slightly longer and uninspiring from what I remember. I suppose the saying is true, Miss Hannah."

"What saying is that?"

"That we all have a double somewhere in this world. On that day, we were all exposed to Eva's. The gentleman that was with her was introduced as her twin brother. He had no resemblance to anyone. That would be the last time I saw the girl in Germany. Her brother... well that's a much different story. Now let me explain how Rainier was one of the most influential people of our time.

"As we all continued to sit in the room with Fuhrer Hitler, Piper began to explain Operation Trading Places. The Fuhrer began to chuckle to himself as he took another long puff of his fine cigar. It was the laugh of undeniable satisfaction. Piper passed out before and after pictures of over 20 men and women that had significant facial injuries due to accidents, birth defects, and the causalities of war. His work was remarkable. I believe even today; he would be considered a great in cosmetic surgery. On his last two patients, he took his research to another plateau by injecting the rexonium agent into the facial tissues. Not only did this radically increase recovery time, but it also negated any surgical scars. You could not have drawn better faces.

"But I was confused, his last two patients were the Fuhrer and Rainer. In fact, both my father and I looked at each other with confusion." The Furher spoke.

"I am sickened by the betrayal of the Russians and the Americans leaders. Do you know why we went to war in the first place? It is because of those dirty dogs. There was no price they wouldn't pay to get their hands on this research... our research. Grade X was more important to them than establishing any type of solidarity. Their greed will cause them pain. A great deal of pain in fact. By tomorrow, everything will have changed. The Nazi party will have surrendered, and a bitter end will have come to the leader and his wife. I can't wait to see the headline… *Hitler dead.*

"Let them marvel at their perceived victory. Let them revel in it like the dirty dogs they are. Victory will still belong to us. Our long-term plan goes into effect now. Rainier and Eva have made the ultimate sacrifice for us all."

"Piper looked at both me and my father and gave us a nod of approval. The Fuhrer took one more long drag of his cigar then swung his chair around to speak with us man to man. If it were physically possible for my mouth to drop to the floor, it would have and then some. I didn't understand what was going on. This was Fuhrer Hitler speaking to us with the same oration and command we had grown to admire. But his face was different. It was much different in fact. He looked just like Rainier. That son of a gun Piper had done it. He really did it."

"So, what did this scientist Piper do exactly, Mr. Marshall? I think you lost me. Why would Rainier pretend to be Hitler?"

"I believe your question should be why did Hitler pretend to be Rainier? What did Piper do you asked? He reconstructed the Fuhrer's face to look exactly like that of Rainer. They were already the same build and height. He miraculously gave the Fuhrer a new identity. And to equalize what was the most critical piece of this puzzle,

Rainier's face was reconstructed to look exactly like the Fuhrer."

"Wait a minute…"

"Hold on for a second, Miss Hannah. I'm almost there. When the Russian soldiers invaded the Chancellery, they found two bodies in the garden. That of Adolf Hitler and the other of Eva Braun. In another correction to history, it was the Russians that doused the bodies with petrol before setting them on fire. Joseph Goebbels got to witness it all. After the bodies burned, the soldiers gathered around and peed on their charred remains. Eva had been dead for some time and was kept in somewhat of a frozen state. The cyanide capsule was lodged into her mouth before taking her to the garden. Rainier Santini gave his life with a bullet to the brain to preserve a future for Nazi Germany."

"So, you're telling me they basically *swapped faces!*? Mr. Marshall please excuse me, but none of this makes any sense at all. You're telling me this trading places nonsense had to do with body swapping?" She begins to laugh. "Surely you can understand my apprehension here. This is way past incredible."

"Oh, I quite understand, Miss Hannah. You should have seen me there, totally confused by all of it myself."

"But wait. Reina and Ranier were said to have come back to the United States after their time in Germany. Are you telling me that *Hitler never died*, but came back to America? What about Reina? What is her angle in all of this?

"Yes, you are correct. Adolf Hitler came back to America. He traveled back with Reina. I will bring this all together I promise. There are lots of pieces to this story."

"So, what happed next?"

"Furher Hitler explained what our long-term plan would be."

Chapter 31

The American Dream

May 1, 1945 Sweden

Adolf Hitler stands and paces in a circle, while maintaining a smile on his face that is unfamiliar and surreal. Heinz Gruber, his father, and Piper Guntalf have become a part of history that will forever change the world. After a night of restlessness and anxiety, they all anxiously await to hear about the new vision from their leader.

"Good morning to you all," said Hitler. "Today marks the first day of a new era for our movement. Before I proceed further, I would like us to take a moment of silence and bow our heads for our brother Rainier Santini. Just as I suspected, the Russians assailed the Chancellery. Those dogs not only found the bodies of Rainier and Eva, but they also burned them. Their lecherous deeds will come full circle. But for now, most importantly, they walked right into my trap. They took the bait hook, line, and sinker.

"I know you are all wondering why you? Where are the others? I shall explain."

There is a knock at the door. Hitler directs Piper to answer it. A soldier requests permission to speak to the officer in charge, not knowing the Fuhrer himself was still alive. The soldier gives his salute and gives a manila folder to Hitler. He makes a hasty exit. Hitler reads the contents of the folder. He slams his fist on the table, startling everyone in attendance.

"Those sick dogs. Those disgusting ingrates. They will pay with their blood. I will make sure it flows freely and frequently. Goebbels is gone! He is gone! His whole family slaughtered."

"No, my Fuhrer," cried out Piper. "What happened?"

"Goebbels wanted to end his life. He could not bear to see Germany defeated. He and his wife did not want to live in a country that would become non-socialist. They were ready to give it all up in my name and in honor to everything that I stood for. In the end, I felt it a price too severe to pay. Knowing we were laying the groundwork for our long-term plan, I wanted his six small children to have a future. He and the rest of those that remained at the Chancellery called a cease fire and surrendered to the Soviet troops. They relinquished their weapons. They did everything those snakes asked."

Hitler continues to read the note from his Chancellery officer Hans Krebs and paraphrases it to the group.

"After those bastards burned and pissed on Rainer and Eva, they ordered Goebbels, his wife, and their children to the same garden behind the Chancellery. The soldiers told the children that their parents would be killed unless they ate the candy. Goebbels and his wife both had gags in their mouth so they could only protest with their eyes and watch as each of their children took a cyanide capsule. They then shot Frau Goebbels in her heart, and the good doctor in his head.

"My Fuhrer, how does this impact our plans?" asked Piper.

"It has no impact on what is to happen. Outside of everyone in this room, only Krebs, Goebbels, and Speer know that the body burned in the garden of the Chancellery is not mine. All my other generals… those that pledged their allegiance to this party. Those that looked me eye to eye and drank blood from my chalice. Those whom I never thought would betray me did just that. They are cowards, they are liars, and they are scum just like those red dogs. They only cared about advancing their own careers. That bastard Himmler had already *reached out* to Eisenhower to make arrangements. Himmler hurt me deeply. But within two weeks, I will have the pleasure of mounting his head.

"I have not lost anything. We… our beautiful home, sweet Germany, shall rise again. America and Russia will pay. The world will struggle to breathe, and at that point, we will snuff away the rest of its oxygen. But just before it dies, we will resuscitate it with our German zeal. They will bow beneath our feet. Mark my words, gentlemen."

"What's next for us my Fuhrer?" asked Otto. "What about all of our research with Grade X? We destroyed so much of our research."

"We could take no risks, Gruber. Russia and the United States will be in for a world of disappointment when they find all this chaos was for nothing. All the knowledge I have is in this room. We shall rebuild. Our research will continue, and guess where? America!"

The men look around at each other in shock. Piper himself didn't know many of the details of Hitler's plans.

"My Fuhrer, with great respect to your will, wouldn't that be an automatic death sentence for us all?" Asked Piper.

"Not at all, my dear scientist. It would be far safer for us there, as we will be able to effectively blend in their false melting pot. The United States is an allied nation. But guess what? We have many allies in the US. These allies have already made flight arrangements for us. We all have places to stay, and jobs to go to. All this under the nose of Truman. Too bad Roosevelt couldn't be around when we arrive. We shall launch our offensive from the home of the greedy bastards that entered this war to flex their military prowess. They had no business interfering. Money and greed is always in the fabric of the blanket that falsely comforts man when he falls to the ground. We are going to tear their heart away from the inside. Then we will deal with the red dogs and the rest of the Jews. The US is the perfect German military base. Their advancements in medicine and technology, though far behind ours, is simply superior to Russia's. This move grants us the best vantage point.

"While we are in America building our new might, our brethren here in Germany will continue to rebuild. There will be many sacrifices made over these upcoming months and years, but our home will be great again. Gruber, you and young Heinz will be critical pieces to this puzzle. Young

Heinz, your contributions to this research will yield a better way and a better world for our people."

"Heil Hitler," said Heinz as he rises. His father and Piper follow suit.

"We fly to America in July. But first, we must make our preparations. Sweden will be our safe haven for now."

Hitler reaches into his brown leather battle fatigued satchel and removes a bottle of whiskey.

"Let us drink to our new future. We will destroy the American dream, then make the rest of the dogs beg us for scraps. We begin now!"

Chapter 32

The Stranger Among Us

The day has quickly given to the tint of darkness, as Brooke and Mr. Marshall have been talking for hours. Brooke moves from feeling like a detective to feeling like she is in a sci-fi movie. Things such as this... events that are so incredible, simply don't happen in the real world.

"Mr. Marshall, you are telling me that one of the world's most insane leaders, Adolf Hitler, left Germany unscathed. You are stating that he came to the US to start a new life with a brand-new face, a lookalike wife, and went on posing as someone else... Rainier Santini, *to be exact.* The corpses that were found in the Reich Chancellery were of the real Rainier and the real Eva Braun? Oh, and he brought some of his scientists with him, along with you so everyone could have jobs and be Americans. Do I have this right so far? Too bad I don't swear, otherwise I would tell you what all of this sounds like. Let's just leave it at BULL... this is the most absolute case of it I have ever heard"

"Please, don't back away from your skepticism, Miss Hannah. Never lose that grit you've developed. I suppose someone in your profession has to look at the story for what it is, and not what you hoped it would be. It is late, and I'm afraid we've talked much longer than I anticipated. I would like to rest now. Do you have somewhere to stay? My home is open to you. I have two spare bedrooms that you may use at your leisure. We can pick up again over breakfast. I will show you something that will ease your doubts."

"Thank you for your kindness and hospitality, Mr. Marshall. And please forgive me for my outburst just a moment ago. I was going to check into a room after I left here. Of course, I was thinking I would have been gone hours ago. If you're extending the invitation, I kindly accept."

"Very well then. I will show you to some of the necessary items, then I'm off to bed. Please make my home yours, Miss Hannah."

The next morning

Brooke awakens to the smell of fresh brewed tea, and another delightful smell to which she is unfamiliar. She freshens up and makes her way to the kitchen, where Mr. Marshall is finishing up breakfast.

"Well good morning, Miss Hannah. I'm almost done here. Please have a seat in the dining room. I made a fresh pot of coffee. It's sitting on the table."

"It smells wonderful in here. What did you make?"

"Ah, you like that do you? It's called Lulu. I won't bore you with the drawn-out story behind the name. It's a breakfast quiche that my wife enjoyed. I made this often. I hope you don't mind, but it's vegetarian."

"Not at all, I really appreciate you going through all of this trouble. Can I help you with anything?"

"Yes, you can, young lady. You can go park yourself in that chair over there. Breakfast will be served soon."

Brooke smiles. "You got it!"

Mr. Marshall and Brooke enjoy a delightful breakfast, as he shares with her how the name Lulu originated. There is still much to discuss, so after another cup of coffee, they both dive back in.

"We stayed under the radar in Sweden until everything started to settle in Germany. The news of Hitler's death circulated quickly. There were many arrests made by the Russians. Many of my comrades would go on to spend months and even years in Russian prisons before they were released. Even his private secretary Traudl Junge spent nearly six months in confinement. The Fuhrer laid out a plan for Piper and my father to continue their work with rexonium. They would further their research with me, in the hopes that an invisible army could be set up within the US. Their other studies would revolve around making the ultimate weapon of mass destruction.

"We all traveled to the US separately. The Fuhrer and Reina arrived first, followed by Piper, then finally by me and my dad. Here's a bit of interesting news. This whole area was owned by us. It was our little German oasis. The Fuhrer and Reina were just up the road. Piper and his wife were just on the other side of his mound. We shared just over 5000 acres between us all. This was the perfect place to start over and rebuild without outside interference. The Fuhrer built a state-of-the-art lab on his partial for Piper and my dad. There were several scientists who were brought in to assist with the research; however, they were kept at a distance in terms of the purpose of the research.

"I was amazed that the Fuhrer had amassed such vast resources and money in a foreign land. I was not very optimistic when we left Germany behind, but everything was coming together. His brilliance once again shined through. He even set up a school for us where we could learn the English language with fluency. A year had passed us by quickly. And it was shortly thereafter where we suffered a major setback. One morning as Piper was getting ready for breakfast, he suffered a major heart attack. He died shortly thereafter.

"The Fuhrer was devastated. There were so many years of research and expertise that could not be replicated. He had the utmost respect and confidence in my dad; however, this was not a one-person operation. Besides, Piper held on to certain secrets as a precaution. This was ordered by the Fuhrer very early on back in Germany. But something else was happening quite troubling. The Fuhrer's health was declining while his paranoia was increasing. He finally yielded to the fact that he was sick. He asked my dad to give him the cocktail of lithium and rexonium that he and Piper had worked on.

"This combination did wonders for the Fuhrer. It almost completely reversed his Parkinson's disease, greatly eased his psychopathic paranoia, and increased his spryness if you will. And this is when things had become even stranger. He turned his focus towards my development, and how the rexonium was having an effect on my cells. He sent away the other scientists and worked exclusively with my dad. There was something they were keeping from me, but I wasn't sure what it was. I just continued to do as they asked.

"Ten years had passed. I continued to assist with research a few times per month. But I had also gone away to college, landed a job with a chemical company... imagine the irony of that, and I married my life-long sweetheart, Janet. My dad was able to see me complete college and attend my wedding. He passed away later that same year. After he passed away, the Fuhrer and Reina up and moved to New York. That was the last time I had seen him. I received a phone call from him just before he passed away in 1965."

"1965!?" Shouted Brooke. "You're telling me Adolf Hitler lived in the United States of America until he was what... in his seventies?"

"That's exactly what I'm telling you, Miss Hannah. But you must keep this in mind. There were only a few people that knew of his true existence. To everyone else, he was a farmer named Rainier Santini."

"OK, so what was your last conversation about?"

"He told me nothing was lost. That the German people would have *Lebensraum,* which means living space. He said everything we worked for was going to be realized, and a new direction had been set in motion. He asked if I could travel to New York immediately. He said he had maybe only days left. I jumped on the first plane available, but I was already too late. He passed away just hours before my arrival. Reina gave me a large package, one that I will share with you."

Mr. Marshall rises and brings back a small banker's box. He removes several folders and gives Brooke a black two-pocket binder.

"I want you to look through this one first," he said.

Brooke flips through the binder of pictures and data, not really sure what she's looking at.

"Can you tell me what this is? What should I be looking for in this binder?"

"That binder is the continuation of Grade X testing, which continued through 1964."

"But you said you lost contact with Hitler long before that. Who was the test subject?"

"Before I answer that, let me explain what you are looking at. That data shoes how rexonium can be fused intramuscular, much like it was done with me. It also shows how it binds and hides itself within the tissue and bone for extended periods between doses. Again, much like the research Piper and my dad did on me. What he was able to achieve was magnificent. Once injected, rexonium could stay in the system for up to 9 months. And not only that, it remains completely undetectable. If you keep flipping the pages, you will see that he was able to bind rexonium, plutonium, and uranium into one substrate. This substrate was injected into the test subject's body with unprecedented results.

"Imagine, Miss Hannah, one person walking around undetectable that could blow up and destroy a large city in moments. Imagine what thousands of these people would do."

Brooke quickly reflects back to her conversation with Mr. Trekker. "Is this what the Ugly Bomb is all about?"

"The Ugly Bomb!? How on earth have you heard of such a thing? That was a foolish poem written long ago. But you know what? That poem was certainly ahead of its time and in some ways quite accurate. Yes... what you have before you is, The Ugly Bomb. But wait a minute. I need to answer your earlier question. You wanted to know who the test subject was, right?"

Mr. Marshall gives Brooke another folder filled with pictures and other information.

"What is this!?" Brooke asked as she shuffles through pictures.

"Keep reading, Miss Hannah. Once you reach the last page, it will all make sense."

Brooke continues to read wide-eyed at what she's seeing.

"Mr. Marshall! This can't be... are you telling me?"

"I'm not telling you, Miss Hannah. I'm showing you. The rest will require some investigative technique I'm afraid. This is what you traveled from Detroit to discover. I hope you are not disappointed."

"What can I do? Is Reina still alive?"

"The last I heard, she was in a nursing home in Manhattan. She suffers from dementia. She is locked down in that place. There is no way you're going to get to her. But then again, you are quite resourceful. Perhaps you will figure out a way. I want you to keep that last folder. If you are successful in getting to her, perhaps those pictures can jog her memory. But if not, I think you know the next step. There are a couple of things I need you to take with you, they go hand in hand with one another. These are hidden research notes from my father and Piper. I didn't discuss them with you, but the message contained is self-evident and powerful. And take these. There are instructions inside on how to use them. Something tells me you'll need them soon."

"I know my next steps thanks to you. Why are you doing this? Helping me I mean. If I expose this information, everything you've worked your entire life for goes up in smoke."

"I, like many followers, loved the Fuhrer's idealism. He captured our imagination with promises on building a utopian world for all German people. But something snapped inside of me after I got out into the real world and met so many classes of people. Many of them I called friends. The killing... all those millions of lives lost suddenly made very little sense to me. One had to be in Berlin in the days and weeks before the Russians invaded the Chancellery. Bodies and their missing parts strewn all over the streets. Men, women, and even children. And then the concentration camps. You've read and no doubt heard the stories.

"He was so far gone psychologically he blamed the Jewish people for everything. His plan would be the eventual genocide of the entire Jewish race. I looked at my wife, and looked at my friends. I said to myself there was another way. I no longer wanted to be a part of his dream. But I am guilty, Miss Hannah. I did nothing about any of this. That is until today. Perhaps the things that I've told and shown you can prevent the end of our beautiful world. I wish you luck, Miss Hannah. I hope you can help us keep it beautiful. This is such an unfair task and request to ask of only one person. But after looking at those pictures, I'm sure you can see time might be running out."

Brooke and Mr. Marshall enjoy lunch together before she hits the road back to the airport and home to Detroit. A simple, yet honest request has turned out to be a race for humanity. Reina Santini might be her last hope to save it.

On the flight back to Detroit, she can't help but to feel a degree of guilt and sadness.

Surely this is nothing more than some crazy story. We as countries would have been at each other's throats regardless. What a pity though. Perhaps one of our best presidents in recent years, may potentially fall flat on his face because of this. Let's hope everyone is wrong.

Chapter 33

Best Friends

April 14, 2017

Through all the busy work schedules and cancellations, Brooke's friends, Agent Lana Quivner and Carla Duclass are flying in to Detroit for a weekend of fun and relaxation. Due to bad weather in Seattle, Carla's flight is delayed a couple of hours. Brooke and Agent Quivner decide to do a little shopping inside the airport and grab a light snack until her flight arrives. This gives them the opportunity to catch up on a few things. But even more, it gives Brooke the opportunity to ask for some help.

"So listen, there's something I need your help with," said Brooke with puppy dog eyes.

"It's about those twins isn't it?" Agent Quivner shakes her head as she smiles. "I know you like the back of my hand. I could tell you were raring up for something."

"Yes, it's about the twins. But it's also about so much more. I have been drawn into something that has dire consequences. I am in over my head this time."

"Girlie what the hell! First off, are you in any danger? Have you received any threats?"

"No, I'm not in any danger. At least not yet. And I have not received any threats."

"What the heck is that supposed to mean? How do twins going to Germany in the WWII era put you in a potential precarious position?"

"What if I told you it could have immeasurable national security implications?"

"What!? How Brooke? You have to give me more. I need to see the full picture. And if it does involve national security, I'm afraid our girl time is going to be cut short."

"Look…here's the thing. I need to do some further validation on all of this information I received at the beginning of this month. I need to be 100% sure of everything before I tell you we need to go guns blazing."

"OK, so this has some potential to be something major, or it could also be a huge bust? You do understand that we need something concrete and factual. With everything happening right now, the last thing we need is more egg on our faces. I need some more information girlie. And what is it you need help with?"

"Well, what would you say if I told you Adolf Hitler died in 1965…not 1945 as everyone has believed?"

Agent Quivner laughs aloud. "Brooke…girlie…please tell me you are not serious right now? Wait a minute, you are serious. How is that even possible? We have remains and DNA."

"Remains were found, that much is true. Do you remember some years ago when they exhumed his remains?

The DNA was inconclusive, and the dental cavity actually belonged to a woman."

Agent Quivner's cheeks turn slightly red. "Well, I suppose I can't debate that. But IF he lived, where did he disappear to?"

"That's what I need to validate. It doesn't make much sense at this point to give you all the details before I validate this information. I suppose that's where I need your help. Sources have verified that Reina Santini is at the Chase Gardens Retirement Community in Lower Manhattan. I need to get access to her. From what I understand, she is under lock and key."

"Wow, so you found one of the twins? She is still living? What about her brother?"

"Her brother passed away some time ago. I really need to speak with her. I was also told that she suffers from dementia. I'm not sure to what degree and which type specifically."

"Reading between the lines, I'm assuming her being under lock and key might have to do with this potential national security threat. Am I correct?"

"Yes. I need to see her right away."

"You are all over the place girlie. Aren't you supposed to be just reporting the news? How in the hell do you get roped up into this ridiculousness?"

Brooke shrugs her shoulders with a completely innocent look on her face.

"Well whatever! OK, give me some time. I will try to have something for you before I leave Sunday morning."

"You are the best Lana. Oh my, look at the time. Carla's flight should be landing soon. We better hightail it."

Brooke and Agent Quivner pick up Carla, and all three of them go out for a relaxing night on the town. After taking in some local sights, more shopping, and another night on the town, it's time for the ladies to say goodbye. Carla had an earlier Sunday flight than Agent Quivner. After they drop her off at the airport, Brooke and Agent Quivner head off to breakfast. The agent receives a surprising call.

"Hello, Agent Malcomb. What did you find out?"

"Well, I have a directory of all the tenants of Chase Gardens. Reina Santini is listed; however, she is part of a no visitor list. It looks like there are several people on this list. Who controls it and why, I wasn't able to ascertain. I don't know if this helps at all, but there was a familiar name on the general tenant list. Ann Parker...she's Mr. CNN, Evan Parker's mom. Reina Santini and the others on that private list aren't in any type of isolation from what I can tell. They just don't accept any visitors. But if you happened to visit Ann Parker...maybe you could have a few words with Santini. Oh and get this, that place costs over $11,000 per month to stay there. This place is very exclusive. That's all I have."

"Wonderful work agent. I believe this is all I need for right now. I'll be in touch!"

Brooke is bursting at the seams hoping the call was in reference to Reina. "Was that about Reina?"

"Yes it was. I have some good news. First off, she is alive and well. But here's the kicker. She and several others are on a strict no visitor list. So there's no way you'd be able to ask for her directly, and based on what you've told me so far, I'm going to have to assume that any activity to do so might raise red flags."

Brooke gives a heavy sigh. "So how can I get in there to speak with her?"

"Hold on there girlie. Here's where it gets interesting. Guess whose mom is also a tenant?"

"Who!?"

"Evan Parker!"

"Evan Parker!? Get out! You are right. It just got very interesting."

"I know how much you loathe him, though you won't admit it. I think this might be the perfect opportunity to make a new friend. All you have to do is play to that tremendous ego of his. How you do it is up to you. This might be your only way in. What do you think?

"Just to set the record straight, I don't loathe him," said Brooke trying not to laugh. "He's so robotic and insincere. I just didn't enjoy my interactions with him the last few times we met. And do you remember what he asked me during that Gainsborough interview? He flippin suggested that my parents physically abused me. I was done after that."

"Yes I remember that. I wanted to smack him for you. But still, you've got to swallow that and jump on this opportunity. So riddle me this. If you are able to get in there and eventually speak with Reina, and she confirms what you believe so far, then what?"

"Then you will be my very next phone call."

"The plot thickens. Have you ever thought about being a writer girlie? Lately your life has been a great example of a suspense thriller."

"Ha ha very funny. Although you make a great point. Wish me luck with my Evan conversation."

Chapter 34

Good Memories

April 22, 2017 8am

Brooke's efforts to reach out to her New York colleague, Evan Parker, from CNN, are successful. She sold him on dropping in to visit friends in the area, and to also do some prospecting for someone from back home. She told him one of the local business owners was considering Chase Gardens. Since she was working on a local story surrounding affluent retirement communities, she convinced him a look around one of the most exclusive communities in the country would provide a finishing touch to her story. It was public knowledge Evan's mom stayed in the community. He always bragged privately how he didn't have to wait the usual three years on the waiting list. His mother was able to move in within six months. They meet at The Roasting Plant on Orchard St. in Lower Manhattan. From there, Evan drives them over to Chase Gardens.

"OK Brooke, I'm just going to give it to you straight. I was devastated I couldn't be a moderator for that first televised presidential debate last year. But please here me out."

As they stop at the red light, he looks over to Brooke.

"No one, and I mean no one could have done a finer job. I tip my hat to you. You have raised the bar for a long time to come. Well, that is until I do it again." They both laugh.

With that admission, Brooke's outlook on Evan takes on a much more positive note.

"Thank you, Evan., That's so nice of you to say. It means a lot coming from you."

"Thank you for allowing me the opportunity to get that off my chest. So, you're writing story on retirement communities back home, huh? Are you going to be doing any new development?

"We may very well be. There are two different sites that are in competition for the building of a state-of-the-art community. I thought it would be great to see a community that always ranks in the top ten best each year. What made you decide on this place for your mother?"

"It was actually Senator Truner. His mother, father, and aunt were all community members. He and I golf together quite a bit. We were talking about some options for my mom when he suggested this place. It's pricey, but I couldn't bear the thought of having her in just any type of nursing home. She deserved the best, and that's what I wanted for her. Boy did she fuss at first. After the first week, she was sold. She loves that place. Well, here we are. She's going to love the company. It's just me and her, so she doesn't get many other visitors. The senator drops by from time to time though."

After pulling through the gated entrance, Brooke is amazed at what she sees. They are surrounded by lush greenery and an 18-hole golf course. There is a full-sized library, a movie theater, and a Starbucks neatly lined up next to one another. The individual living quarters resemble condominiums. Brooke is quickly able to see where $11,000 a month goes. It's 9:30 am and the residents have just finished their buffet style breakfast. As usual, many of the ladies make their way over to the arts and crafts center to continue their conversation. This is where Evan takes Brooke to meet his mother before going on a tour of the grounds.

As he enters there are many happy faces beaming with joy to see him; however, none are brighter than his moms.

"Hello my beautiful ladies. How is everyone doing this morning?"

Everyone speaks in scattered cadence, "Good morning, Evan."

"And here is my lady. Hello mother. How are you doing today? Did you have a good breakfast?" He kneels down and kisses her on the cheek.

"They fed us exquisitely as always, son. And who do we have here? She's very pretty!"

With a look of embarrassment. "Umm, mother I'd like you to meet, Brooke Hannah. Brooke, meet my mom, Mrs. Parker."

"Well, it's a pleasure to meet you, Brooke."

"Likewise, ma'am. Evan and I are fellow reporters. I work for WDIV in Detroit."

"Oops. Forgot to mention that," said Evan somewhat bashfully.

"From Detroit!? So, what brings you to these parts?"

"I'm here visiting friends and looked up Evan to catch up."

"Yes, mother, they might also be building a community similar to this one. I thought I'd give her a quick tour."

"What a nice idea. You will love this place, Brooke. It feels like I'm on vacation each day I wake up."

Evan looks down at his phone. "Please forgive me I have to take this. It's urgent. Please continue, I will be back in a few." He quickly exits to take the call outside.

"That happens a lot," replied Mrs. Parker. "But I suppose that's what makes him who he is with the network."

"Oh yeah, I've had to apologize to many friends and family for the same things. It definitely comes with the job. So, it looks like you've made lots of friends here. Everyone seems so nice."

"Yes, I have. I know every single resident here by name. I also know their life story and what they want to be when they grow up. Well almost all the people. There are a few that have some illnesses, so they are in and out."

"I know someone that may still be a member here come to think of it. Well, I should say that I don't know her personally. It's more an acquaintance of an acquaintance."

"Sometimes that's how the best friendships start. What's her name? Surely I can tell you if she is still here."

"Reina is her first name."

"Oh dear, you mean Reina Santini? That poor soul. She is the nicest and sweetest person you'd ever meet. She's battling Alzheimer's. But boy is she giving it the one-two punch. She has her days. Sometimes she thinks I'm her mother. But it's ok. She's as cute as a button."

"Is she here now?"

"Yes. If you turn around, you'll be looking dead at her. She's reading the newspaper. She loves to read every single word in that thing from front to back. When she is having her good days, she is the trivia queen. She knows everything! I think today is one of her good days. Go ahead and say hello to her. I'm sure she'd like that. She only gets one visit a month, though none of us ever sees who it is. Strangely enough, she won't tell us either."

Evan quickly reenters. "Brooke and mother. Please forgive me, but this is going to take me a bit longer. Maybe another 15 minutes or so!?"

"Take care of whatever you need to, son. Brooke and I are doing just fine."

Evan smiles as he retreats back outside. Brooke decides that it's now or never.

"Would you excuse me for a moment, Mrs. Parker? I think I will go over and say hello to Reina. Since this is one of her good days, perhaps it will make for some pleasant conversation. I shall return so we can continue with ours."

She approaches Reina to introduce herself.

"Umm hello there. How are you?"

Reina moves her newspaper aside and gives Brooke a once over as she smiles at her.

"And who are you?" her voice is soft and forgiving. The gentle wrinkles in her face yield to a once youthful beauty. Her hair is meticulously crafted into a silver bun. Her body is frail but able.

"My name is Brooke… Brooke Hannah."

"Well, it's a pleasure to meet you, Brooke. I'm going to have to say you're too young to be living in this place. Are you here visiting?"

"Why, yes I am. Do you know Mrs. Evans over there?"

Reina turns to her right. "Oh, you mean Ann. Yes, of course, she is such a nice lady."

I came here to visit with her son, Evan."

"Oh, that's not her son silly girl, that's her husband. I think he's working on taking her out of here."

Brooke's heart drops. She knows Reina believes what she's saying. She also knows there's a chance Reina won't remember anything about Hitler.

"Umm yes ma'am that's my mistake. Does your husband come by to visit you too?"

"Heavens no. My husband died years ago."

"I'm so sorry to hear that. How did he die?"

"He passed away in his sleep. No, that's not right. He died of a heart attack."

"Again, I'm so sorry to hear that. What was his name?"

Reina picks up the newspaper as if it's going to help her with the answer. "I'm sorry young lady. I don't remember his name. That's strange!"

"No, not all, Miss Santini. Here I have something I want you to look at."

Brooke removes a folder from her tote purse and looks around before opening the contents. She places several pictures in front of Reina.

"Is that your husband Miss Santini?"

"Oh my... will you look at this. He was always so handsome in his uniform. Yes, that is my dear husband. Where on earth did you get these?"

"Wait... look at this one Miss Santini, you were so beautiful."

She shows her a picture of her and Hitler standing with their dog at the Reich Chancellery.

"Oh dear, we were such a wonderful couple. I don't remember that picture, but there he is again in that handsome uniform."

Knowing time is of the essence. "What about these Miss Santini?"

Brooke lays out the remainder of the photos, consisting of three pictures. As Reina looks at the pictures, tears start welling up in her eyes.

"Look at him. He is so precious and sweet. Isn't he handsome?"

"Yes, he is Miss Santini. What is his name? Is he still living?"

"Have you taken a liking to him? Of course, he's still living. But he's also married. I hope that didn't sting too much."

"No not at all Miss Santini. What is his name? Where is he now?"

"I wanted to name him after his dad. Wait a minute, his dad's name was Richard. I remember now. He never liked the name he was born with. He changed it to Richard. Isn't this wonderful Brooke? I can remember." She picks up the pictures of Hitler.

Brooke smiles nervously. *Are you kidding me? Of course this is wonderful news.* "Do you remember what he changed his name from?"

"Well yes I do --- wait a minute. On second thought, I just can't seem to remember. I'm confused, and I'm not quite sure why. But he never liked his birth name."

"OK, Mrs. Santini, please look at the other pictures too. Can you remember? What was his name?"

"I think that's supposed to be a secret, Brooke."

"He seems like such a person. I sure would like to know his name."

"Hmm. You seem like a really nice girl. I suppose I can tell you. But wait a minute, I think I should whisper it to you. That way, you and me would have our own secret right? Well not really a secret. It's just kinda of fun that way don't you agree?"

"Yes, absolutely. It's a conversation with my new friend," said Brooke as she leans her ear over to Reina's mouth. What she hears nearly makes her pass out.

"Oh my! Oh my! That is a really good conversation." Brooke hands are shaking as she places the pictures back in the folder. "Miss Santini, I have to go now. I promise I will come back to visit again. I have to take these pictures, but I will bring them back again, OK?"

"You are such a sweet girl. Please make sure you come to visit me again soon. I enjoyed your company. I will make sure I let everyone know my new friend stopped by."

"NOO! I mean, that won't be necessary. I want it to be our secret!"

"I love secrets. Very well! We will keep this one just between us two."

Brooke makes her way back over to Mrs. Parker and bids her farewell before making a hasty exit where she finds Evan just outside the door.

"Brooke, I was just about to pop back in. I'm all done now. Is everything alright? You look like you just saw a ghost."

"Something just came up for me too. Can you get me back to my car? I can take the tour another time."

"Sure, no problem. Let me say goodbye to mother."

Brooke turns and stairs into the clouded sun. "That's all the proof I need."

Chapter 35

New Jersey Drive

E van drives Brooke back to her car at the coffee shop. She makes trivial conversation, which throws him off from asking any unnecessary questions. As he drives away, she realizes she has created a new ally. The information she received from Reina makes her end game clearer, yet the steps to get there are what evade her. She knows now is the time to bring her friend Agent Quivner into the loop as this is now official business. She makes the agent her first call when she enters her vehicle.

"Well, hello girlie. said Agent Quivner excitedly. "How did you do? Any luck? Are you and Mr. CNN best buds?"

"Wow …and you call me the drama queen. You know I have to admit; he is not really such a bad guy after all. And I don't know about that best buds mumbo jumbo, but I can certainly say we are friends now. But Evan is the least of my concerns right now."

"Oh boy. So, by the tone of your voice, I'm assuming you found what you needed?"

"Yes, I did… in a very big way. I need to see you right away. Are you in Jersey right now? Can we meet?"

"Umm yes… absolutely. Meet me at my townhouse around 5:30pm. Would that be fine? You do still know how to get there, right?"

"5:30 is great. I need to check my emails and call my station manager for a personal day on Monday. My flight leaves late Sunday night, so I think I'm good there. I'm still in downtown Manhattan, so it'll take me a couple of hours to get to you."

"OK, I have a few questions for you. On a scale from 1-5, with 5 being severe, where would you say this new information you have places things?"

"A solid 6!"

Agent Quivner sighs deeply. "Are you safe right now? I can arrange for a detail to follow you here."

"I'm safe. I don't believe anyone is on to me yet."

"What do you mean yet!? OK, just get here right away. And you didn't mention anything to Evan, right?"

"No, of course not. I wouldn't want to involve anyone else in this mess. I'll be on my way soon. And if you have some merlot, I'll gladly take a glass. Probably the bottle at this point."

"I am well stocked. Be safe and call me if you notice anything out of the ordinary on your travels here."

Brooke turns her car into a quick virtual office as she makes all the necessary arrangements and tends to her pending commitments. Agent Quivner has created a mild paranoia in her mind, as Brooke is constantly checking her rearview and side mirrors in nervous accordance.

Brooke's drive from Manhattan was much smoother than expected. She arrives a few minutes ahead of the agent. Brooke calmly exits her vehicle as the agent pulls up. They greet each other happily with hugs, knowing the purpose of this visit has both of them on edge.

"Come on in, girlie, and make yourself at home. You really have my head swimming, so why don't we just jump right into it if you don't mind."

"Not at all. There is a lot to cover. I must warn you though… this information is way out there and difficult to believe. But please know it's all true. I'm not quite sure where I should even start."

"How about telling me about the twins, and then how it's possible that Hitler died in 1965."

"Sure! They are intertwined with one another. If you don't mind, I'm going to give you all of the surface details, so you know where I am so far. We can then do a deep dive."

"Fair enough. Let her rip!"

"Reina and Ranier were part of an underground network of Nazi sympathizers. They were recruited by Hitler himself for two important purposes. The first was that Reina looked identical to Eva Braun. So much so that not many could tell them apart. Eva died over a year before her body was burned in the Reich Chancellery. She had been frozen all that time. Just before the Russians overtook it, they placed a cyanide capsule in her mouth to make it look like suicide."

"Brooke!? Alright I'm sorry keep going. This is already insane."

"I know it is. I'm just starting though. Rainer was the same stature as Hitler. He made the perfect candidate."

"Perfect candidate for what?"

"For the ultimate plastic surgery. Yes, way back then, the Germans had the know how to do some magnificent work. Hitler and Rainier basically switched faces and identities. The person that was placed beside Eva was actually Rainier Santini. Hitler was able to return to the US with Reina because everyone thought that he was someone else."

Agent Quivner has a stone look on her face. "I want to laugh, but I know you are so dead serious right now. How could something like this happen? Where did you get all of this information?"

"I will share that with you in a moment. Have you ever heard of a project called Grade X?"

"No, it doesn't sound familiar. What's it about?"

"It centers on a chemical that the German's created sometime in the 1930's. They were working on creating a super army and the ultimate weapon of mass destruction. As things got out of hand in Germany, Hitler continued his research here in the US."

"OK, but according to you, he died in 1965. What happened to the research? Why is this a threat now?"

"Well, that's just it. The research never stopped. It continued to a point where it was ready for deployment."

"So, we have some German spies on our soil that are attempting to start a nuclear war? Is this what you're trying to tell me?"

"No, not exactly. As far as spies, I don't know about that. I do know that his network is still alive and well, and has probably grown exceptionally in size over the years. I don't know what the intent is, but I know someone who does."

"Who!?"

"Someone that might share his same ideologies ...*his son*!"

"His son!? No girlie... no. This can't be right!"

"Reina whispered it to me herself. She didn't remember what her husband's name was at first. When I showed her pictures of Hitler, she instantly lit up. She knew they were together, but she still couldn't remember his name. When I showed her the last pictures, that's when she remembered everything. Take a look at these."

Brooke shows the agent the pictures of a young boy, some of them taken with Hitler and Reina.

"He looks like an ordinary boy. I'm not sure what you want me to see. I suppose I can see some similarity to Hitler, but this was too long ago. What's his name? He's still alive I take it?"

"He is very much alive. His name is Simon... Simon City... President of The United States."

Agent Quivner quickly rises as she gives each picture a closer look. Her heart is beating so fast that it begins to scare her. She calms herself, though at this point unable to speak. She excuses herself from Brooke with no words, only a hand motion signaling that she would be right back. She goes into the kitchen and returns with two wine glasses and a bottle of merlot. Her voice is now even-tempered and peaceful.

"So, you're telling me one of the most atrocious people to ever walk this earth had a son. And you're telling me that his son is our president. The President of the United States is a Nazi?"

"I don't know whether he is or not, Lana. I have lots of things for you to look through. We might need to do a grocery store wine run for another bottle."

"Don't worry about that, girlie. Like I said over the phone, I'm well stocked. Show me what you have."

Chapter 36

The Ugly Details

Brooke tells Agent Quivner how this whole odyssey started, from the request from Hans Albrecht, to the pictures she received from Mr. Marshall. Brooke states her story with conviction; however, Agent Quivner is still struggling to accept the facts. Both ladies know this has become something quite complex, with the potential to be a highly dangerous threat.

"I have to give it to that bastard Hitler," said the agent. "He was brilliant... in fact for more brilliant than anyone obviously knew. So, it sounds like he came back with this Reina lady because he was so fixated and in love with Eva Braun? I realize you don't know the answer to that, but that's one of the many signs of a psychopath."

"As sickening as that sounds, you are probably right. He couldn't live without Eva, so he found a replacement. If he didn't find someone that looked just like her, I'm sure he would have used his crazy team of scientists and doctors to reconstruct someone else to accomplish the job. I wonder if he ever loved Reina, or did he only see Eva? But enough of that. I don't know what to do now. I knew I needed to rope you in, but where do we go from here?"

"Girlie, this one is a doozy. You've just placed on my lap one of the most egregious and amazing historical misalignments this world has ever seen. Stories like this may never happen in entire lifetimes. This news… these facts are so over the top there's not much I can do with them."

"What do you mean? Why can't you? What am I missing? I just gave you everything I had."

"Hear me out for a moment. You originally told me this had the possibility of being a national security incident. With this news you've given me, it is that times one hundred easily. We aren't talking about the average businessman or congressional person. We aren't even talking about the most affluent crooks. This is about the *President of the Flipping United States.*

"You don't just take down the president. And to mire this is the utmost complexity, you're talking about a president that may have been planning a major catastrophe for many years. This is a classic case of the clown behind the makeup. We have never seen his true face. Once it's revealed, we have to be ready.

"The president has an abundance of power, and many departments that ultimately fall underneath him, including mine. It sounds like he already has countless hidden allies both here and abroad that might be ready to implement anything at a moment's notice. Based on everything you've shown me, I'm not so sure who the good guys are anymore. If we involved the wrong people in this, it could backfire with dire effects. It sounded like Mr. Hans Albrecht was starting to talk about production before he passed away. I wonder what he meant."

"That's what's most frustrating, not knowing what the true threat is, and when it might be launched. If it's a nuclear weapon of some type, what are our options?"

"Well, I'm going to guess this falls totally outside of normal protocol where you need a number of individuals involved in the final checks and balances system to ensure you really want it to go boom. If President City is controlling this underground somehow, all it might take is his word alone. I don't know what our options are. I would like to say neutralize the president, but that won't happen without involving others that might be privately sympathetic to whatever his cause is."

"Wait! That's it!" shouted Brooke excitedly as she paces the floor. "Do you remember that box I told you about? The one that Mr. Marshall gave me?"

"Yeah, I do. What about it?" Agent Quivner looks at Brooke with confusion.

"I think you're right. We need to neutralize the situation. Now I just need access. And you know what? I think I know the way."

"Here we go again, girlie. Something tells me I'm not going to like this idea of yours one bit."

Agent Quivner is at first skeptical as she listens to Brooke's plan. She realizes this might be their only chance. After they finalize the details, Brooke flies back home to solder up the loose ends. She uses her newly gained fame and influence to persuade her station manager to let her and Charlie attend the Global Climate Summit in Paris.

Chapter 37

Welcome to Paris

May 29, 2017 AC Hotel Paris Le Bourget Airport

The city of Paris is bustling with tourists, lovers, and powerful world leaders. Springtime is always special in this city. Paris is a paradise for culture buffs, with an abundance of world-class museums, art galleries, and cultural events, not to mention the outstanding monuments, the literary cafes, and the boulevards that still retain all the romance and charm of the 20's. Located within Le Bourget Airport, the AC Hotel Paris Le Bourget Airport is a four-star hotel that is the perfect accommodation to attend one of the most important climate control meetings in recent times.

Each country has sent their leader and a delegate to discuss a solution for a problem that plagues the world. During this three-day conference, the world leaders will discuss many topics relating to the global climate change. During the first half of day one, leaders from the United States, Great Britain, and Germany speak in brief segments to members of the press.

Brooke and Charlie have taken in some impressive sights in their brief stay in the city. This summit has drawn an unprecedented amount of journalists. This is easily the most journalists she has seen at an event, even eclipsing the Simon City acceptance speech. Thankfully for Brooke and Charlie, some of her fame has spread internationally, as they are able to maneuver their way into the main area where the leaders are speaking. President Simon City has just taken to the microphone.

"Hello to you all, and welcome to Paris. Listen, I'm going to make this brief. Global change has been happening everyday of our lives. This is one of those inevitable changes that will occur no matter what. The reason we're here during these next few days is to discuss how we as a society have altered that inevitability. We have not only changed the dynamic, but we have also changed the timetable, and have done so at an alarming rate. We need solutions, and we need them now. Rest assured we are all putting our differences aside to find it."

The president takes a final pause giving the signal to the press that he is open to take questions. Brooke and Charlie have struggled to get into a good position for the past half hour. These journalists are much more aggressive than she is used to. She settles for a position within shouting distance.

"Mr. President, Fern Rothschild BBC. Was this meeting here in Paris a direct result of your closed-door climate change meeting with Prime Minister Banely shortly after your inauguration?"

"Great question Fern, and no it was not because of that meeting. This meeting was being put into place early last summer. It took some time to get everyone to commit. This is the first time we've had every leader in attendance as a show of solidarity. When I met with Prime Minister Banely, we were discussing details on similar strategies… those that we're going to discuss during this summit. Next question!"

There is a litany of questions coming from every area. Something captures President City's attention. A lone reporter in a canary yellow blazer with a matching 1920's vogue type hat. Brooke smiles knowing the president has noticed her and appreciating her station manager's advice on standing out amongst this turbulent crowd. She raises her hand.

"Ah, a familiar face. Miss Brooke Hannah. From WDIV in Detroit, correct?" All eyes turn to Brooke.

"Thank you, Mr. President, that is correct. I have one question. How does the current climate change affect Grade X?"

The room goes completely quiet. "Oh boy!" said Charlie as he focuses the camera on the president.

Many continue to give her a blank stare, wondering what she is talking about, before turning their attention back to the president for a response. The president is miffed by the question and despondent. He whispers something in the ear of one of his secret service agents and quickly exits the microphone, amongst many pleas and questions being shouted. The room is confused and irritated. Several reporters turn to Brooke looking at her in displeasure. Fern Rothschild from the BBC News walks up to her.

"What the hell was that all about? Whatever Grade X is, it looks like you rather pissed the ole boy off."

"I have no idea. I'm not sure why…"

"Miss Hannah, I need you to come with me," gestured the secret service agent. "The president would like to speak with you."

"Fine. can my cameraman, Charlie come with me?"

"That won't be necessary. He only requested you."

"Don't worry Brooke, I'll be right here waiting for you when you're finished. Give my best to the commander in chief."

The agent leads Brooke to a closed meeting room where the president is waiting.

"Well, hello, Miss Grade X," said the president. "Why don't you come in and have a seat. This should be interesting. I'm going to have some fresh squeezed orange juice. The Parisians do an awesome job with their oranges. Can I interest you in a glass?"

"No, but I'll take a bottled water if that's possible."

The president motions to the agent, as Brooke nervously sits down across from him. He watches her every move.

"You know, Miss Hannah, you really threw me for a loop back there. For the first time since I was a little boy, I was completely tongue tied. Nothing intelligible would form in my mouth. But not just that, I had a total mental block. And guess what? In this age of social media, I'm sure the whole world has seen that by now. Grade X you say? Hmph! How about this, let's cut straight to the chase. There's no need to be cute or coy with one another. What do you know about Grade X?"

Brooke wonders what she should divulge at this point. She decides to play it safe.

"There's not much I know about Grade X. It's something that might be key to this climate situation, correct? Can you tell me if the scientists are still working on a formulation that might be able to counteract the negative effects of global warming?"

President City smiles and leans back in the high back leather office chair.

"I'm giving you one more time to insult my intelligence before I up and leave, Miss Hannah. Grade X is known by very few people. It has always been that way. And when I say always, I mean over 80 years. If you don't believe me, just ask Barnaby Trekker. Oh wait, he died right!?"

The sound of Mr. Trekker's name sends a chill down Brooke's back.

"How do you know about, Mr. Trekker?" asked Brooke nervously.

"Well let's see. Barnaby Trekker was curious just like you are. He put his nose in places it didn't belong. He should have just stuck with running that damned museum."

"You killed him!? You're responsible for his death?"

"Come now, Miss Hannah. We both know he died from a massive heart attack. He wasn't exactly a young man. Since my men have already confirmed you're not wired, *and yes*, I already checked, I'm going to say this. He had a choice to die the way he did, or my way, which would have been somewhat messy. It's really too bad though, from what I hear, that museum could have used a little color to brighten it up. My favorite color is red by the way. Anyway, I was able to find out some shall we say… interesting information from my man on the job after he died. But I'm sure there's much more I'm not privy to."

Brooke quickly thinks back to the call she received from Kyle the day after Mr. Trekker had the heart attack. She wonders if he has any ties with the president.

"I know you two had some conversations, Miss Hannah. We've been watching him over the years. Something must have struck his chord recently because he came snooping around in Germany. It's wonderful to have so many ears to the ground. Since you brought up Grade X, I can imagine what your conversations were about. But alas, your information is limited. That old fool gave himself too much credit. The rabbit hole runs much deeper than he ever knew."

"How deep does it run, Mr. President? What is this all about?"

"You see that's the thing that really burns me, Miss Hannah. You stick your nose in something you are completely ignorant to. If you were anyone else, your ride would have ended long ago."

"And since it didn't end, I'm assuming you have a need or purpose for it to continue for me."

"There is indeed a purpose Miss Hannah. And as much as I like this banter, I'm afraid I'm going to have to cut it short. I have a meeting with the joint chiefs, and then the Russian President… *that should go over well*," he said sarcastically. "Tomorrow morning 6am,same place right here. I will tell you the real story."

Brooke leaves the room and finds Charlie waiting for her in the same spot.

"What in the hell did I witness? What is Grade X? Did the principle give you a paddle? Boy you should have heard the conversations going on after you left. Everyone took to the internet and made phone calls regarding this Grade X stuff, and guess what? A fat goose egg. Everyone is making fun of your perceived gaffe. You will probably make someone's news highlight reel of journalistic blunders. Just as soon as they were in a frenzy to make a connection, they quickly moved on to something else. BUT… they don't know Brooke like I do. That whole thing was no gaffe or blunder, was it? What have you gotten yourself into now?"

"You know me well, Charlie, and there's no way around it. No, it wasn't a gaffe. The truth is, I don't really know what any of this stuff is. I can promise you one thing. I will get to the bottom of it."

"Brooke, this is a whole different ballgame. I don't know what you are thinking about getting involved in but hear me out. The president and his massive entourage of people have power and influence that is way above our heads. I'm sure you already know this, but sometimes as a journalist, you have to walk away from certain stories. Whatever this is all about, I'm sure it's not worthy of the possible onslaught of mental anguish someone in City's position can administer. Please let this one go."

"It was never my intention to walk towards this story. I was lassoed into it. And now, here I am in Paris chasing something. But please rest assured of one thing, Charlie. Everything I'm doing right now has to be seen through. I'm in way too deep to just walk away from it. You and I have had some of the most personal conversations in my life. But this time pal, I have to leave you clueless. I promise I will take good care of myself, and this time I have some help. Please forgive me, but that's as much as I can share right now. But you know me!"

"Yes, I do. A couple of weeks from now you're going to be all over the news for discovering the president is actually Batman." They both laugh. "Look, just keep your promise of being safe and no solo missions please. You know I have your back whenever you need it. Now, are you sure you don't want to talk about this?"

"We just did Charlie. Let's go to that café we rode past on the way here. I would love a croissant and some orange juice. This might be the best time to go. I believe everyone else is getting ready for the UN Secretary's comments. I'm thinking we can skip out on that part."

"Let's do it!" remarked Charlie as they head off for some food and sightseeing.

Chapter 38

The Big Bad Wolf

6:00am the next morning

Brooke makes her way to the same conference room from the previous day and is met at the door by two secret service agents. They both look her up and down, obviously using some type of thermal technology through their dark Ray Ban glasses. They allow her to enter where the president awaits her.

"Good morning, Miss Hannah. Promptness... I love it. You'd be amazed how many people take such a thing for granted. Its super early, and I know you probably didn't have breakfast, so I brought in something lite for you. Please help yourself, I'm going to be doing a lot of talking."

On a short table next to the entrance door, there are fresh pastries, croissants, and orange juice. Brooke chooses her two favorites from the previous afternoon. She takes the clamp out of her bun and lets her hair down.

"I hope you don't mind, sir. I went a bit too tight with my bun this morning. Something tells me I'm going to need to be as relaxed as possible."

"No worries at all. Please, relax and enjoy. So, Miss Hannah. I have a long and challenging day ahead of me. Everything starts going bonkers around 9:00am. I'm going to give you a couple hours of my undivided attention. I'm going to be forthright and completely honest with you. I'm asking that you do the same. With that being said, I want to start by asking you a question. Do you know who I am?"

Brooke postures herself. She's not sure where this is going to lead; however, she realizes the president may already know the true answer to the question. She errs to the side of cautiousness.

"With all due respect Mr. President, I'm not really sure who you are. Is that something you can clear up for me?"

"I suppose that's a fair enough response. I absolutely can clear up any questions or misconceptions you might have; however, I have more questions. Did you visit a woman by the name of Reina Santini? Think carefully before you answer that question. Remember, honesty will buy you the information you've been looking for."

"I did visit her." Brooke is trying her best to look reserved, as she sips some orange juice.

"Do you know who she is?"

"She is your mother!"

The president looks at Brooke and smiles. His eye contact is calculating and uncomfortable.

"You are correct Miss Hannah. Reina Santini is my mother. I suppose in answering that question, you've answered so many others. The main one being, do you know who my father is? And judging by the look on your face, I can see that you know the answer to that question, or at the very least, it is the one thing you are most confused about. I would ask how you found my mother, as well as how you obtained information on my father; however, that answer is crystal clear, as there is only one other living person that knows, and that's Mr. Heinz Gruber. Oops, I forgot, he's a retired farmer that goes by the name of Johnny Marshall. I'm sure he probably gave you an earful if he was so kind to tell you about my mother."

"Mr. President, please."

"Don't worry, Miss Hannah. No harm will come to him. He's an old family friend. His contributions to our society will go down as some of the finest in our hidden world history. So, tell me something. How did you become involved in this hunt for my personal background information?

"I am still asking myself that question almost daily now, sir. It was a personal request from Hans Albrecht. He called me to his home just before he died. He told me The Ugly Bomb must be stopped. He reached out to me because he believed I could do something about it."

The president leans back in his chair laughing hysterically. The nervousness that Brooke felt quickly left her body and started turning into rage. She quickly adjusted her disposition. This meeting with the president is much too important to lose her head over.

"I'm glad you find it amusing Mr. President; however, it's the truth."

"With all due respect, Miss Hannah, you're just a damn reporter. What in the hell are you supposed to be able to do?"

"Well, I'm here before you for some reason, sir. Since you and I are being completely open with each other, can you wipe away my confusion on this whole matter? What is an ugly bomb, and what things don't I know?"

The president rests both hands behind his head before he rises and looks out of the smoke-colored window.

"Very well, Miss Hannah. I will do just that. Two very important and equalizing things happened in 1965. We lost one of the greatest leaders and men our world has ever known, my father, Adolf Hitler."

Brooke adjusts herself in her seat trying not to look pale. Part of her was always hoping the information she had been piecing together was still inaccurate. She is coming to grips with the fact that the son of one of the most ruthless men of our time, now stands a few feet away from her.

"The second most important event during that year, the equalizer if you will, was my birth. Let me ask you something, Miss Hannah. When you were a child, did you go outside to play? Did you have many friends?"

Brooke slightly hesitates. "Well, sure I did. I was outside often. There were many families with kids my age, so I had lots of friends to play with."

"Well, it wasn't the same for me. I suppose I understand what some celebrities complain about that started off entertaining at a young age. They have no life. They have no sense of childhood. Everything is work, rehearsing, and more work. But it was even worse for me.

"I have to give it to my father. He had everything laid out and planned to exact precision. I had each day of my life laid out for me for the first 16 years of it. We stayed in New York. We occupied the two top penthouse levels of the Wildershire. The bottom penthouse was the living quarters for me and my mother. The top penthouse was like a high-tech library. There were over 800 books arranged by due date on every single inch of wall space. In the center of the room was lab equipment and a bed. There were three scientists and two different scholars that worked there daily.

"My father put together a series of live audio and video tapes that I listened to and watched many times until I completely understood the lesson, and I had committed them to memory. These I always watched and listened to in the corner of the penthouse while wearing headphones. My father's instructions were simple. The information was for my eyes and ears only. Once I was done with each tape, I destroyed and burned them. I had classroom types of instructions each day, seven days a week. The two scholars aided me in learning every single one of those books that lined the walls. I read anywhere from 50-60 books a year. On Sunday afternoons, my mother would take me for a walk and ice cream.

"That was as much entertainment as I was going to get during my adolescent years. Once I turned 13, I had the same structured schedule, with the exception of now having a personal fitness instructor. I was allowed to join a gym, and that's when things really started to take off for me. I was working out 4 – 5 days a week, and I had begun some experimental training in the penthouse lab. I spent maybe an hour a day on that hospital-type bed. For the most part, I felt as strong as an ox, though there were days that I didn't feel quite so well. These were usually the days when the scientists wanted to experiment with some different dosages or serums. It wasn't until my 16th birthday, when I watched my father's last video communication, that I understood everything. You wanna hear something cool? My mother kept that videotape hidden until my birthday."

"So, your father died before you were born. Surely you heard about all the things he did. What did your mother have to say about any of this?"

"We'll get to my thoughts on my father in a moment. As I mentioned before, everything was laid out for me each day. What time I woke up, what time I ate, what time I went to sleep. Everything happened in a certain order. My mother and I had our chats late in the evening and on Sunday's when she took me for ice cream. The only thing she said about my father was how much she loved and missed him, and that I reminded her of his greatness. I didn't watch television or listen to the radio until well past my 16th birthday.

"I apologize for interrupting you, sir. What did the video say?"

"I think I will save that one for last. I'm on a roll here, and this feels quite liberating. Do you realize that I have *never* had a discussion with anyone about the things I'm telling you right now?"

"No sir, I didn't know that. I do appreciate your candor."

"Yeah, I'm sure you do. Anyway, being homeschooled certainly had its advantages. At 17, I took my college placement exams and blew them out of the water. As you may know, since you've been snooping around, I attended New York University and graduated summa cum laude with the perfect 4.0 GPA. The only reason I attended college in the first place was to obtain the requisite degree and to place my name out there as one of the best. It certainly worked. I began working with Daimler Copland shortly thereafter. I must say that college was quite liberating. It was my first time being around so many people. I learned about a litany of other cultures and personalities through the people living them. For the first time in my life, I had friends... real friends. But something else happened, which leads me to the question you asked about what I thought about my father.

"I learned that the world is self-absorbed and full of shit, please excuse the French. You media people are something else I swear. All the lies and inconsistent stories about my father floating around out there. My father was a genius and in a class of his own. Now, I will also admit that my father was one crazy son of a gun, especially in his later years. But his contributions were overshadowed by the media's greed to ostracize him."

"So, are you saying it's the media's fault that Adolf Hitler, your father, did all of those unspeakable things? You are talking about the annihilation, by his order mind you, of well over 6 million Jewish people. How is the media responsible for that? How is the media responsible for *Mein*

Kampf? The things he discussed were irrational. These were not things the media planted in his mind. These were created of his own accord. How do..."

"I think you should *slow down*, Miss Hannah. You are talking about the one person that I truly looked up to. Did all of those Jewish people have to die? Maybe and maybe not?"

"Sir, with all due respect, you're talking about innocent lives. You're talking about children... young children. They lost their lives. They never had a chance to grow up and make a difference. All those people had their dreams snuffed away in one horrific instance. Are you telling me you condone this? I refuse to believe that. There is no way the person I interviewed and saw skillfully debate to win the White House is the same person before me now defending such atrociousness."

"I see this topic has really got your blood boiling now. This is the side of Brooke Hannah I'm sure not many get to see. Listen. when I got to college, and since then, I have made many friends in almost every culture. I have met people that are trying to make a positive difference in this world and make it a better place. I have also seen the other half, the one's that disgusts me the most. I want you to work with me here for a moment.

"Nearly two years ago, right here in Paris, we had a group of individuals carry out terrorists' activities and killing many in the process. What about 9/11 and the World Trade Center? Hey, just last month in Chicago 17 people were gunned down execution style in a gang war retaliation. I can sit here and go on and on. Let me ask you this Miss Hannah, do these things disgust you?"

"More than I can possible describe, Mr. President."

"So, in my examples, we go from philanthropy and promise, to disdain and hopelessness. But even with all the hope and money in the world, it can't stop the other from happening. Do you know why?"

"Why sir?"

"Because we lack effective leadership. My father had designs on making an ideal world for all German citizens. I wish you could have seen the full-scale model that Albert Speer built. It was breathtaking. My father had it placed in our penthouse where I would marvel at it each day. In one of the videos he made for me, he laid out in delightful detail how each building and structure would revitalize our people. He was going to use the same blueprint throughout Europe, and then throughout the rest of the world. But because of the treachery of the bottom feeders, he was never able to realize his vision. But that's over now."

"It's over!? What do you mean it's over?"

"Miss Hannah, this world needs a leader right now. Someone who can be deliberate and decisive. Someone that can rule fairly and firmly, but most importantly, someone who knows what the future looks like. The world needs me right now. Someone who's not afraid to blow the house down!"

"I see. So, first you become the president, then you become the big bad wolf!? Haven't you seen this scenario fail miserably repeatedly? The people, even the bottom feeders as you call them, will never allow this to happen. You are far too intelligent not to realize this."

"The world, or should I say *logical world*, doesn't want a tyrant, Miss Hannah. The world needs a savior right now. Think about it. No more worries about gun control, no more worries about terrorism, no more worries about abortion, no more bickering political parties. There will be no slavery, no illegal sweat shops, and no more illegal drugs. You can continue to go to school and work in the job of your dreams. The list of benefits are tremendous. You will finally be able to behold utopia in your lifetime. Your parents will be able to enjoy it. Your kids one day will flourish in it. Culture, the arts, peace. isn't this what you want? Please be honest here. I am the only solution that can provide this."

"What I can't believe is that I'm having this conversation with you, Mr. President. I guess I finally understand the phrase of the clown behind the makeup. Now respectfully, I'm not calling you a clown by any means. But you are showing me now everything I've seen over this past year has been completely superficial. You've been hiding behind the makeup of a savior, when what you actually want to do is be a destroyer. A destroyer of ideas of societal means.

"Logically, it doesn't make sense to me. This is nothing you will be able to implement. People will rebel. I'm not talking a few people; I'm talking about the majority of the population won't agree with this."

"Ahh, that's really quite simple, Miss Hannah. Those that don't agree, and those that choose to not to yield to the obvious solution *will be exterminated*. And I mean every single one of them. I have taken every possible measure into account. I'm prepared to do whatever is necessary to create the place my father has always dreamed of."

"Mr. President please. Everything that you've worked for. All the relationships and friendships you've built. Please think of those people. You don't want to throw that away. Whatever you are planning it's not too late to stop it. You want a quick history lesson, sir? You are the most popular president in the history of this world. You are Time Magazine's Man of the Year. You won the Nobel Prize for peace before you were even elected. The world admires you right now. You don't need a dictatorship. All you need to do is to continue leading in the way that you are. You are making unprecedented history right now. Just continue with being the man that you can be, not what your father wanted you to be."

The president starts clapping. "Very well done, Miss Hannah. I can see a future in politics for you. That was powerfully stated and impactful. Unfortunately, it's just not going to sway me. You see, I got to know my father on a very personal level without ever physically being in his presence. He taught me things about the world and about myself that have proved to be extremely valuable each day I walk this earth. I am becoming just what I want. This has been a plan in the making for many years. The light of day is almost here. Now, let's talk about that video my dear father left for me on my sweet 16.

Chapter 39

Genius Activity

B rooke continues to listen intently to the president. She is determined to sway his way of thinking. She believes there's still a way to his heart.

"He told me that everything he did was for the people," said the president. "He knew there was a way to a better life, and that's what he wanted to bring to Germany. He never wanted to influence matters by war. In fact, just before the breakout of WWII, he had signed a secret peace agreement with the United States, Russian, and Japan. Had he not been stabbed in the back by Stalin and Roosevelt, things would be much different for everyone.

"Had that agreement stayed in place, my father would have ushered in a new era for the German people. He was willing to share everything, even the science and engineering behind his greatest secrets."

"Regardless of what Russia or the US did, he provoked the war. And then he took it a step further with the mass annihilation of the Jewish people. They had nothing to do with him being backstabbed."

"As I stated earlier when you asked what I thought of their annihilation, I said some may have deserved it, and some may have not. This is the only area where my father and I see things differently. He was fixated on the Jewish people. He thought they were conniving and untrustworthy. He wanted them all gone. He felt the world would be much cleaner without them. In fact, he really didn't care much else about any other race outside of his own, yet he was willing to tolerate them, except the Jews, to further beat that point into the ground.

"He told me about Grade X and the advancements that were made with it. He also told me something that his earlier scientists never knew. You see my father was bi-polar. The only treatments they were experimenting with back then was lithium. Piper created a blend of several chemicals along with rexonium and lithium to aide my father with his condition. But he wanted more, you see.

"My father was a workhorse. He wanted Piper to create something for him that would also allow him to work on minimal sleep. Something that would increase his mental awareness and keep him sharp. Against Piper's warning, he wanted to test a beta drug on my father, but he was a stubborn man. He took the speed type supplement and mixed it with the bi-polar medication. He did it for several years. And guess what? Zero side effects. But that would not be the case for long. He became delusional at times; some might even say psychotic. The mix in medications had indeed caused irreversible side effects that weren't evident early on. But through his greatness, he was still able to lead until the very end."

"With all due respect sir, are you giving him a pass for his actions because he received some bad medicine? If he had never taken any of it, would it really have changed anything?"

"It absolutely would have. The timetables would have been adjusted, and his mastery would have been able to be seen through in a much shorter time span. He and Albert Speer had drawn out the designs for all of Germany. Too much time was wasted."

The president looks at his watch.

"I haven't much time left. I will continue my story about the video if you can stop being so combative and become more appreciative of this gift."

Brooke is stone faced and unimpressed. "Please continue, Mr. President."

"Thank you. My father also told me what the purpose of my experiments were. I was receiving injections of rexonium and multiple other compounds. They were testing to see how long it would stay in my body and the impact it would have at extreme temperatures. My research was different than what was performed on the first test subject, your friend, Mr. Johnny Marshall aka Heinz Gruber. They injected rexonium with other forms to create strength, speed, and recovery. My purpose was to create stability and impact. Impact being the key word.

"Previous nuclear bombs were quite heavy. Some of them up to 20,000 lbs. It was impossible to transport a huge cache of warheads of one bomber plane. My father and his scientists had already mastered using rexonium with nuclear warheads. But here's the beauty of rexonium, it can do mind-numbing damage with a fraction of the weight.

That means you can carry that full cache of bombs on one bomber plane. When rexonium was initially used to manufacture my father's first bomb, he nicknamed it Fat Man because of the aftermath that would be left in its trail. That name should sound familiar to you, Miss Hannah, because the United States stole it. They gave the name to the bomb that was dropped over Nagasaki. Nonetheless, I already have enough of these bombs manufactured to influence any conversation.

"But the most intriguing research had to do with the effects of rexonium in the body. Four ounces of the rexonium special blend can stay in the body for up to 72 hours completely undetected before it eventually passes through the pores or through urination. Now get this, when the body is either injected with rexonium, or it's consumed in liquid form, small neurotransmitters are scattered throughout the body. These neurotransmitters react to a message sent via one of these things."

The president removes his watch and places it on the table. Brooke cautiously looks on.

"The middle point on the watch activates a special frequency. The frequency causes the neurotransmitters to give the body a mild shock. This causes the rexonium to have a violent reaction usually within five seconds. The body heats up quickly to well over 700 degrees Fahrenheit causing a massive explosion of the body tissue. By the time the body explodes, it has already been reduced to tiny, fragmented particles that create spores, which flow through the air. Anyone that makes contact with these spores will die within ten seconds. The radius of one blast from a human body can send spores at least a mile before they combust and evaporate harmlessly.

"And now you know all there is to know Miss Hannah. But there is one question I neglected to answer. What is The Ugly Bomb? My father's last instructions on that video tape was to ensure I destroyed the animals that tried to take everything from our people. He asked me to ensure the United States and Russia were brought to their knees. *I am the ugly bomb*, Miss Hannah. Just like I told you. One day, I will make the world explode. But fear not, I'm not going to sacrifice myself or let anything happen to me, I mean, who would lead us? I have a great alternate.

"Nooo, please! You can't! What are you planning to do, Mr. President?"

"You will find out tomorrow. Feel free to join the festivities when we make our grand announcement. Oh, and don't worry, you're completely safe. I spiked your orange juice with a special rexonium cocktail that will make you immune from the blast."

"You son of a …"

"Now, now. Please don't be ungrateful, Miss Hannah. I did this because I can see you going places. You are one of those in the upper percentile. I think you would make a welcome addition to the team. Oh, and if you intend to have that cameraman of yours with you, I advise you to take him a glass of that too."

"Please Mr. President I…"

"Will you look at the time? I'm afraid I have run out of it. I was just starting to enjoy myself. Whether I see you tomorrow or not, the world is about to change. I will be in touch."

The president makes his exits as Brooke sits there unable to move.

"I've failed," she mumbled to herself. "I have let everyone down. What can I do?"

Her phone vibrates alerting her to a text message. As she looks at it the message from Agent Lana Quivner asking her to call, she does so immediately.

"Hello Girlie," said the agent. "Since you answered, I'm assuming you have a few moments."

"Yes, I just finished my conversation."

"Then tell me, is it green or red?"

"It's red. it's very red."

"Dammit! I need you to meet me now."

"I can't Lana, remember? I'm in Paris."

"Umm yeah, so am I. Room 111 in your same hotel. Bring Charlie with you."

"Wait, what!? OK never mind, I'm on my way!"

Chapter 40

Teamwork

Brooke quickly grabs Charlie and heads to Agent Quivner's room. Charlie is alarmed at her erratic behavior; however, he knows he's about to get answers to something he probably doesn't want to know.

"It's this room Charlie," motioned Brooke with her head as her hands are both full. "Can you knock please?"

"Umm sure." Charlie only has to knock once as Agent Quivner quickly opens the door.

"Come on in you two!"

"I'm so glad to see you, Lana. Here take this and the other one is for you Charlie."

"Orange juice!" said Agent Quivner and Charlie at the same time.

"Yes, orange juice! I will explain in a minute." Brooke gives Agent Quivner a hug.

"It's nice to see you again, Charlie."

"Yes, same here. But why here? What's going on you two? Does this have to do with that Grade X question you asked yesterday, Brooke?"

"OK, so Brooke, let me help you out here. Charlie, I know Brooke has probably told you very little about this situation and with good reason."

"Wait Lana, before you start did you," Brooke begins to whisper. *"Did you check the room for bugs?"*

"We are good to go, girlie. Have you forgotten what I do for the bureau? This room is clean as a whistle. We can speak safely."

"Oh boy," said Charlie. "This is about to be good."

"Charlie, the reason I came is because we have an international security risk. If we don't act quickly and intelligently, many lives may be at risk."

"Dear God! OK, what do you need me to do? What's the risk?"

"It's way too much for Brooke and me to go into detail right now. All I want you to do is keep filming regardless of what's going on. More than likely, you will be the only person able to do so."

"Wait, there are hundreds of camera people here. Why would I be the only one capable? Never mind!"

"I believe sometime during tomorrow's announcement is when all of this is going to come to a head. If that's the case, based on what intelligence we already have, there will probably be only one live feed, and that feed will show us only what they want us to see. I need you to show us the real story. And lastly, I need Brooke there to report all of it. I have secured an off-network live feed channel for you. You will have the world as your stage at hopefully the right time."

"Lana, do you think this is too dangerous for us to be so close?" asked Brooke.

"No, not at all. Did you read those last files you gave to me?"

"Honestly, no. I skimmed through them but didn't see anything of relevance."

"Well, you didn't skim well enough. Take a look at this."

Agent Quivner grabs her briefcase and retrieves the file that Mr. Marshall gave to Brooke. She turns her attention to the last two pages which gives the summary notes. The more Brooke reads, the wider her eyes get.

"Are you serious!? Do you think this is true?"

"After weighing everything carefully, I believe this data is accurate."

"Well, I don't want to take any chances. I want you and Charlie to drink that orange juice. The president gave it to me and politely said it's laced with some type of rexonium agent that should counteract the effects of whatever he plans to do."

"Wait, what!?" Shouted Charlie. Who or what the hell is rex err, whatever you said? I'm not drinking that."

Brooke picks up the glasses of orange juice and gives one to the agent and the other to Charlie.

"Charlie, I want you to be able to go back home to Lori in one piece. Now *drink* the damn orange juice!"

"Alright, geez!" he and the agent drink it down. "Hey, it tastes like regular juice. That wasn't so bad after all." Brooke looks at him shaking her head.

"OK, girlie, the special announcement takes place tomorrow noon," said the agent. "Charlie, business as usual tomorrow. I want you to capture the action from the back of the room. There shouldn't be any problems with you setting up there. I will give you all the information you need in the morning to patch into the private channel. Now, if you can give Brooke and me some time, there are some loose ends we need to tie up."

"No problem. I will continue shooting some video for our local coverage feed later. You two be careful."

"Thank you, Charlie. The same to you. I believe this thing will be over soon."

Agent Quivner and Brooke catch up on all the details of the conversation with the president earlier. They go over the details on how the next day will play out several times. If they miscalculate in even the least bit, it will spell disaster for many.

Chapter 41

4 Eva

8:30am the next morning

Brooke, Charlie, and Agent Quivner meet in the lobby of the hotel to go over final arrangements before they head over to Le Bourget to hear the big announcement. Everyone is expecting some sort of agreement or language on global climate control; however, to what extent is what everyone is waiting for.

"Well, don't you look bold and powerful in your navy blue and pinstripes, Miss Girlie girl," said the agent.

"Thank you, chickie. Maybe you won't be able to see my heart beating through it so easily."

"Everything will be fine. No worries. And how is Mr. Cameraman Extraordinaire doing this morning?"

"I'm doing well Lana, and I'm ready, I guess. The good news is I don't know completely what I'm ready for. I suppose it's all for the best."

"Good. Here take this." Agent Quivner gives him a piece of folded paper. "That will get you access to our secure hidden network. I want you to patch all of your feeds directly through that link."

"You got it!"

"Alright you two, its show time! We're almost there, Brooke."

11:30am

Charlie has completely set up at the rear of the conference center. As Brooke enters the room, she is quickly greeted by a familiar face.

"Good morning, Miss Hannah. It's so nice to see you again."

"Mr. Marshall!? What on earth are you doing here?"

"Please tell me that the information I gave you was quite helpful."

"Yes, Mr. Marshall, it was indeed helpful. But why are you here? Is it about the summary section of the notes you gave me? Are you sure…"

"I am 100% sure they are accurate. I'm here to fulfill my last obligation. All these years have passed me by, Miss Hannah. I have had some really good years. It's a shame to have it end this way, but my dues must be paid. I made a promise I must keep."

"What are you talking about, Mr. Marshall? What promise and to whom did you make it? I don't understand."

"The Fuhrer told me one day I might be instrumental in taking this world into a new era. I am the original test subject. I'm also the sacrificial proxy for our great president. My body is imbued with so much of this Grade X chemical that sacrificing myself right here today would fulfill the promise. This is for Eva, the only person or thing he ever truly loved. My death will most certainly ensure President Simon City will be the new ruler of all."

"But wait, you said the data was accurate!? What are you doing?"

"I'm sorry, Miss Hannah. It was a pleasure to meet your acquaintance."

Mr. Marshall walks away and down the aisle to a seat near the front of the room in the VIP section. Brooke quickly looks for Agent Quivner. She calls her on her cell phone.

"Hey, what's up girlie? Is everything OK?"

"No.... Hell no! He's here. I just spoke with him. He is the ugly bomb. We have to get everyone out of here now." Brooke tries to keep her voice low, but her movement and facial expressions cause some to notice.

"Whoa, Whoa! Who are you talking about? Who showed up?"

"Mr. Marshall is here, you know, Heinz Gruber. He says he is fulfilling some type of last destiny. I think he's going to blow this place up. All the world leaders will be gone. Only the president will stand. Gruber... He's the original ugly bomb."

"Wait, hold your horses. Even if he is, the data. What about the data?"

"I don't know... I don't know."

"Ladies and gentlemen, we are ready to begin." The announcement reverberates from throughout the room.

"What do we do Lana?"

"Trust the data. It's too late now. We have to pray its right. I hope that orange juice was legitimate. Hang back with Charlie. I think we'll be fine."

The Secretary General opens the third day of the conference with his thoughts and comments. In an unusual order of speakers, the President of the United States comes up to the podium next.

"Ladies and Gentlemen, traveling dignitaries, members of the press, and all. Welcome to our third and final day of this remarkable conference. This is unprecedented. We have over 180 countries represented here today. During these past three days, we put away our egos, put away our differences, and came together under one accord to draft what are the most comprehensive and exhaustive policies on global climate control ever. What we have drafted is certainly not the panacea for all our climate woes. The truth is we still have much work ahead of us. What this agreement does so effectually is giving us the blueprint to establish a foundation. One in which we can continue to forge ahead. With this accord…"

A man quickly rises from a front seat on the aisle. The president stops his speech in mid-sentence as he points to the man, but it's too late.

"HEIL HITLER… HEIL EVA BRAUN!" The man raises his hand in salute to the Fuhrer. As the Secret Service Agents take the president down to the ground and cover him, the president pushes the middle button on his watch. Within two seconds, there is a loud and deafening explosion. Everyone takes cover on the floor and Brooke,

Agent Quivner, and Charlie duck. He still has the camera rolling. While everyone else is on the floor in panic, the three of them quickly realize there is no blood, and no one appears hurt. There is just a mild yellow haze that circulates throughout the room. As they look toward the podium, they see the president has been taken to safety.

"It worked… it worked," said Brooke as Agent Quivner makes her way over.

"I don't like this yellow cloud floating around the room," said the agent. Everything looks fine so far, but I want to make sure it's not the orange juice helping us out, versus this whole thing being bogus. Charlie, go back to your camera and get all this footage. All the other frequencies and connections are offline. You are the only one live right now. Brooke, you need to do your thing. The world is watching right now. You need to calm them down. I'll take care of the president."

Brooke and Charlie, the dynamic duo, goes live and brings the world up to speed on what has just transpired. The room is in absolute chaos as very few people are moving from the floor. The yellow haze continues to linger.

Meanwhile, Agent Quivner uses her radio to speak with another agent.

"Agent Garros, is everyone alright?"

"Yes, Agent Quivner. The Secretary General and the rest of the world leaders have been moved to safety."

"Is the president there?"

"No, they have already moved him back to the hotel. He is quarantined in his room."

"Perfect! I'm on my way."

Agent Quivner makes her way to The AC Hotel Paris Le Bourget Airport with a detail of French Police. The room to the president is lined with Secret Service Agents.

"Hello, I'm Agent Lana Quivner FBI. It's urgent I speak with the president about the latest developments."

The Secret Service Agent disappears inside the president's room. He reemerges and shows Agent Quivner in along with the four French Police.

"Agent Quiver, correct? What the hell happened back there? Is anyone hurt? Did they apprehend the person responsible for this?"

"I apologize for the slow communication, Mr. President. All our server lines were taken offline. This job was as professional as it gets. The good news is the person that's responsible will no longer be able to harm anyone. He blew himself up."

"Dear God! How many are injured? How many casualties?"

"Zero, Mr. President. There are no injuries other than some ripped pants and skirts from hitting the floor so quickly."

"What do you mean!? Didn't you say the man blew himself up? If a bomb went off so closely, how are there no casualties? I don't understand." The president is frantic.

"You don't sound happy about that sir. Everyone is fine. Here take a look at this."

The agent patches into the security camera remotely where the world leaders are being safely held. She shows it to the president. He immediately turns pale.

"I don't... I don't understand!"

"Wait a minute, Mr. President. I believe Brooke Hannah is live right now from the scene. Do you mind if I cut on the television?"

The Secret Service Agents and French Police look at each other confusedly. Agent Quivner turns on the television and it immediately shows Brooke live at the scene. She turns up the volume so everyone can hear it clearly.

"Again, there are no serious injuries. The person responsible for the explosion has not been identified at this point, but it has been confirmed that he died in his foiled attempt. Wait, I have the Secretary General here with me now. Secretary General, what do you have to say?"

The agent shuts off the television. "There's one more thing, Mr. President. Something I'd like everyone to listen to. It's an excerpt from your interview with Brooke Hannah yesterday."

"What excerpt? I didn't have an interview with... *wait a damn minute*. Agent if you want to keep that title, I recommend you stand down."

"With all due respect, Mr. President, I will not. Everyone, please listen to this. By the way, Brooke was quite happy you allowed her to let her hair down yesterday. It looks like you did the same."

"That hair clip... *that damn hair clip*. I don't..."

Before the president can say another word, Agent Quivner presses play on her portable recorder and places it on the table.

"Very well, Miss Hannah. I will do just that. Two very important and equalizing things happened in 1965. We lost one of the greatest leaders and men our world has ever known, my father, Adolf Hitler."

"So, your father died before you were born. Surely you heard about all the things he did. What did your mother have to say about any of this?"

Miss Hannah, this world needs a leader right now. Someone who can be deliberate and decisive. Someone that can rule fairly and firmly, but most importantly, someone who knows what the future looks like. The world needs me right now. Someone who's not afraid to blow the house down!"

"Should I continue to play the rest, Mr. President?"

The president stands and turns towards the window. His agents take off their glasses. They look displaced and muddled. The French Police stand at attention, not knowing what they should do.

"Tell me what happened, Agent Quivner. Let's be on the up and up," asked the president.

"It appears many years ago your father's scientists Piper Guntalf and Otto Gruber changed the formulation of rexonium. They could not live with placing something so powerful in the hands of your father, for he had lost his mind. He was a paranoid psychotic that would probably have destroyed the planet. The chemical properties were changed to mimic the original. When Heinz Gruber or Mr. Johnny Marshall as he was recently known, decided to blow himself up, the only thing he did was vaporize his body. There may be a few hurting eardrums from those closest to the explosion, but everyone will be just fine. All your formulations, wherever you are hiding them, are completely bogus. It's over, Mr. President."

"This man, the President of the United States, is Adolf Hitler's son?" asked one of the French Police.

The president turns around. "Yes, he was my father and one of the greatest examples of what a true man should be fashioned after. I have failed him. My father's closest friends betrayed him. And now it looks like the same has happened to me. This world will never recover. This world has no tomorrow."

"The world will be just fine, Mr. President. You'll have a long time to watch it happen."

"Not in this lifetime agent." The president reaches into his pocket and quickly swallows something.

"No, No, No! shouted the agent. "That's cyanide. *Get it out of his mouth now.*"

Before the agents could react, President Simon City collapsed to the floor dead. The clown without makeup has closed his eyes for the last time.

Epilogue

One week later

A gent Lana Quivner and Brooke are meeting at the bureau's office in New York. So much has transpired in a very short period of time.

"The world is going to be in a great deal of shock for quite some time," said the agent. The vice president has done a remarkable job of keeping the government together and keeping the world close. She is going to do great as our new president."

"Did you get the official confirmation from the Secret Service and the French Police?"

"I did indeed. The incident is officially moved to the black hole never to see the light of day. President Simon City died from a heart attack in his hotel room. He was the second confirmed casualty. The bomber was never identified, so Mr. Marshall can truly rest in peace."

"Thank you, Lana. If this whole affair where to get out."

"Trust me, Europe doesn't want to relive anything from those dreadful years, and the United States would never recover from such embarrassment. It is buried as it should be. But there's two more pieces of information I want you to know."

"Sure, what is it?"

"It's about Albert Trekker."

"Mr. Trekker!? What did you find out?"

"Well, the French were feeling a little generous and shared some top-secret info. Your sweet old guy was more than a holocaust survivor and museum manager. He worked for Interpol, and was involved in a high-level case tracking Hitler."

"What!? What do you mean? Are you saying he knew Hitler was alive all this time?"

"That's the piece he was never able to confirm. When you were contacted by Hans Albrecht, it gave Mr. Trekker another person to help solve this mystery. He was feeding you all the information he could without revealing himself to you. Simon City found out who he was and put a hit out on him. It appears the hitman may have had a soft spot because it was never carried out."

"The surprises never stop. All this time I had no idea. You agent people are good at what you do," Brooke said as she smiles.

"And so are you, girlie. I did mention I had a couple of things to tell you."

"You sure did, I'm bracing myself. Let me have it."

"It seems our president was not very good securing his own personal data. We are working through the records; however, we may have found the entire underground cell of Nazi sympathizers. We are going to put this entire thing to bed. The Bureau has the support of multiple law enforcements sources throughout the world on this one. They don't need to know who the information came from."

"Great work, Lana. I really appreciate everything you've done for me. I have no idea how to repay you."

"Well, for starters, you can plan the next trip. Speaking of trips, you said you were going to spend the weekend in Florida. What's up that!?"

Brooke looks up and blushes. "*I did mention* he was kinda cute right?"